THE TIME MACHINE

H. G. WELLS

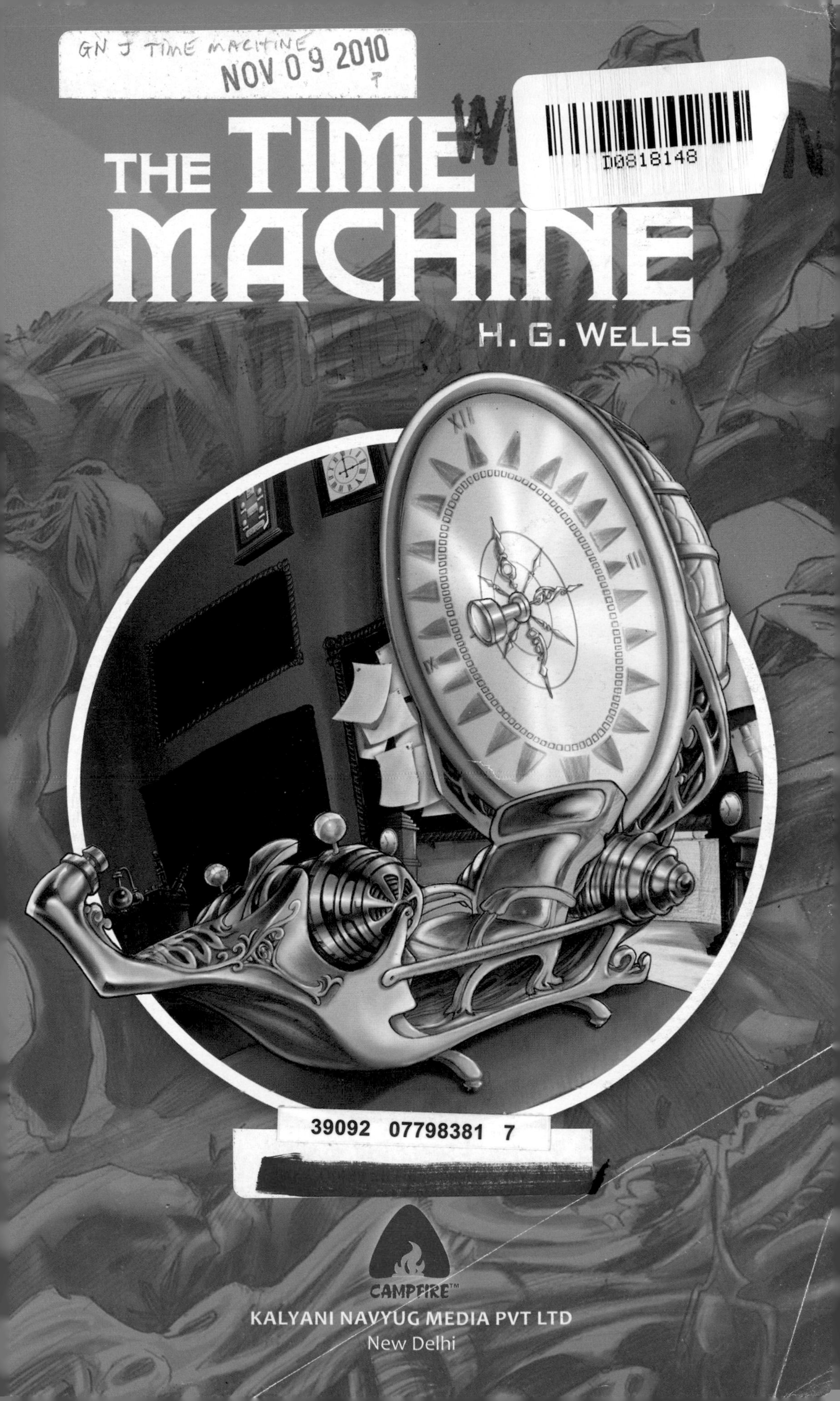

CAMPFIRE™
KALYANI NAVYUG MEDIA PVT LTD
New Delhi

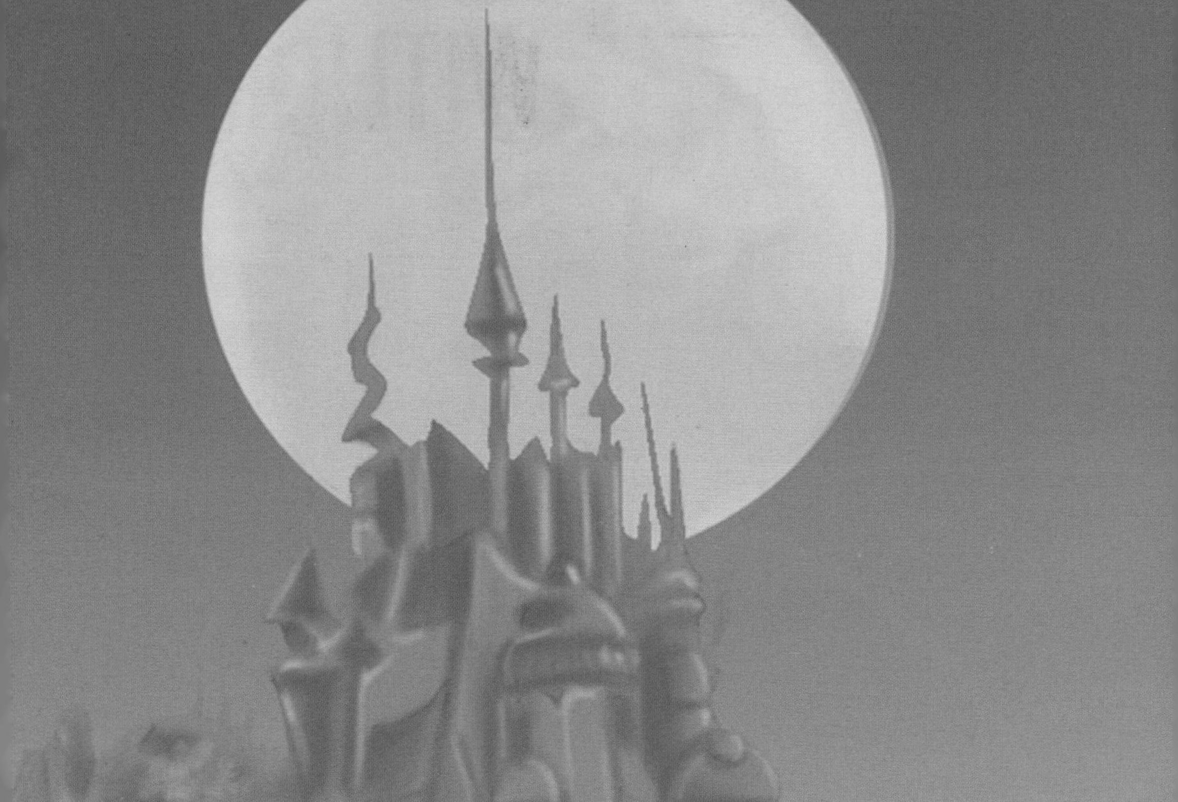

Sitting around the Campfire, telling the story, were:

Wordsmith	:	Lewis Helfand
Illustrator	:	Rajesh Nagulakonda
Colorist	:	Manoj Yadav
Color Consultant	:	R. C. Prakash
Letterer	:	Vishal Sharma
Editors	:	Eman Chowdhary
		Andrew Dodd

Cover Artists:

Illustrator	:	Rajesh Nagulakonda
Colorist	:	Rajesh Nagulakonda
Designer	:	Manishi Varshney

Published by Kalyani Navyug Media Pvt Ltd
101 C, Shiv House, Hari Nagar Ashram
New Delhi 110014
India
www.campfire.co.in

ISBN: 978-93-80028-26-2

Printed in India at Rave India

About the Author

Considered one of the pioneers of science fiction, Herbert George Wells was born on September 21, 1866 in England. He was the son of domestic servants who later became shopkeepers. Wells always had a great passion for reading, but with his family struggling to make ends meet, he spent much of his youth shuttling between school and a series of odd jobs. He did everything from working as an apprentice to a draper, to acting as an assistant to a chemist.

At the age of eighteen, Wells joined The Normal School of Science in Kensington to study Biology. Here he was taught by T. H. Huxley. This was a crucial period of his life as it had an immense influence on his writing.

Wells received a Bachelor of Science from the University of London in 1888, and began to teach. He enjoyed writing stories and articles alongside his day job, and gradually moved into writing on a full-time basis. He married his cousin Isabel Mary Wells in 1891.

The year 1895 was a turning point for Wells, both personally and professionally. It was the year he left his first wife and married a former student, Amy Catherine Robbins. It was also the year when his first major novel, *The Time Machine*, was published.

Still considered one of the greatest science fiction novels of all time, *The Time Machine* was the first in a string of successful books in which Wells's unique take on unusual subjects came to define certain genres. His tales of alien invasions in *The War of the Worlds*, invisibility in *The Invisible Man*, and eugenics in *The Island of Doctor Moreau* have influenced generations of writers.

While most famous for his work in science fiction, Wells worked on a variety of genres. An advocate of social change and member of the British socialist group, the Fabian Society, Wells spent much of his later years writing about his views on politics and society, and even offered predictions about the direction in which the world was headed. H. G. Wells continued writing until his death at the age of seventy-nine in 1946.

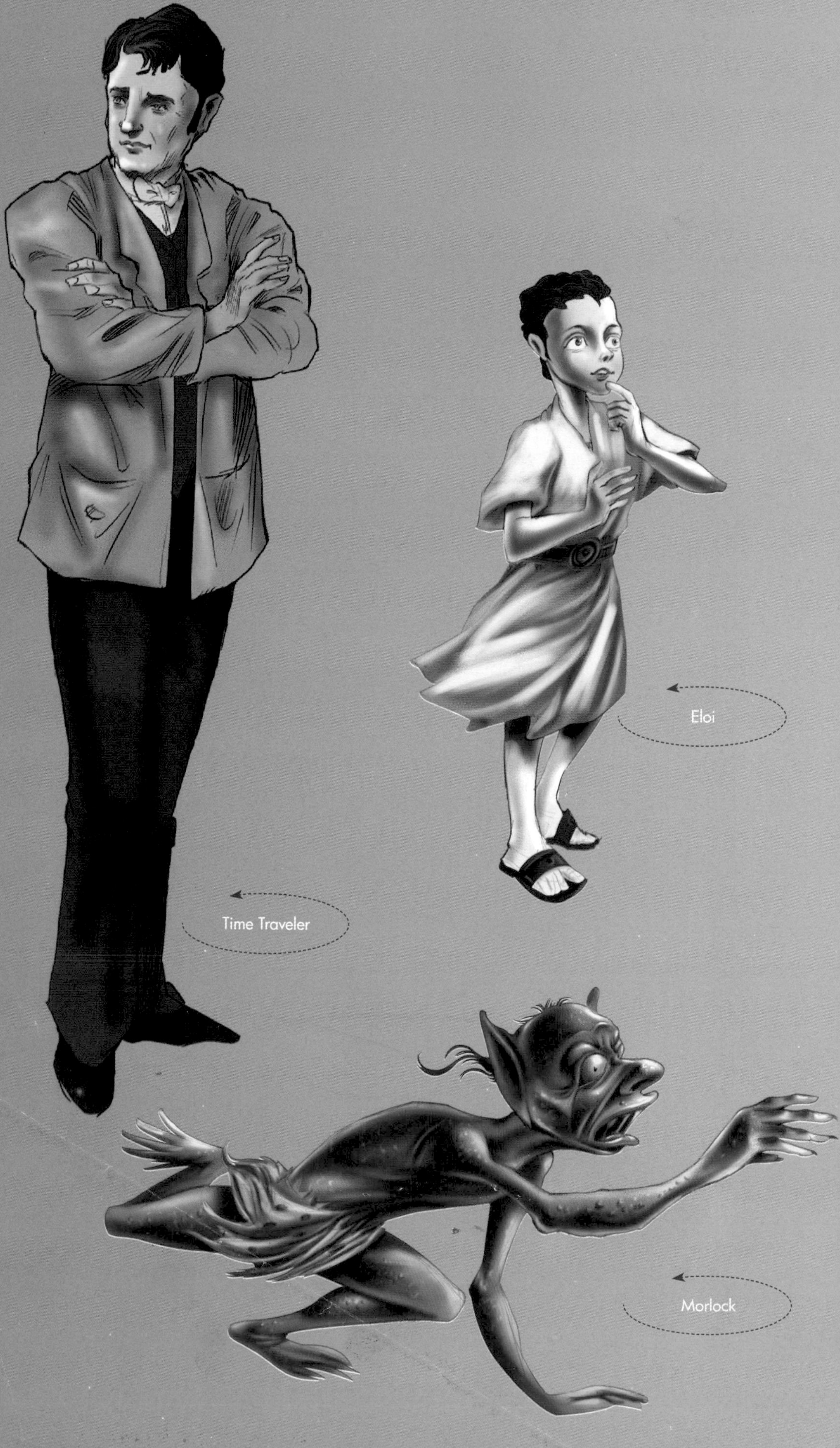
Eloi
Time Traveler
Morlock

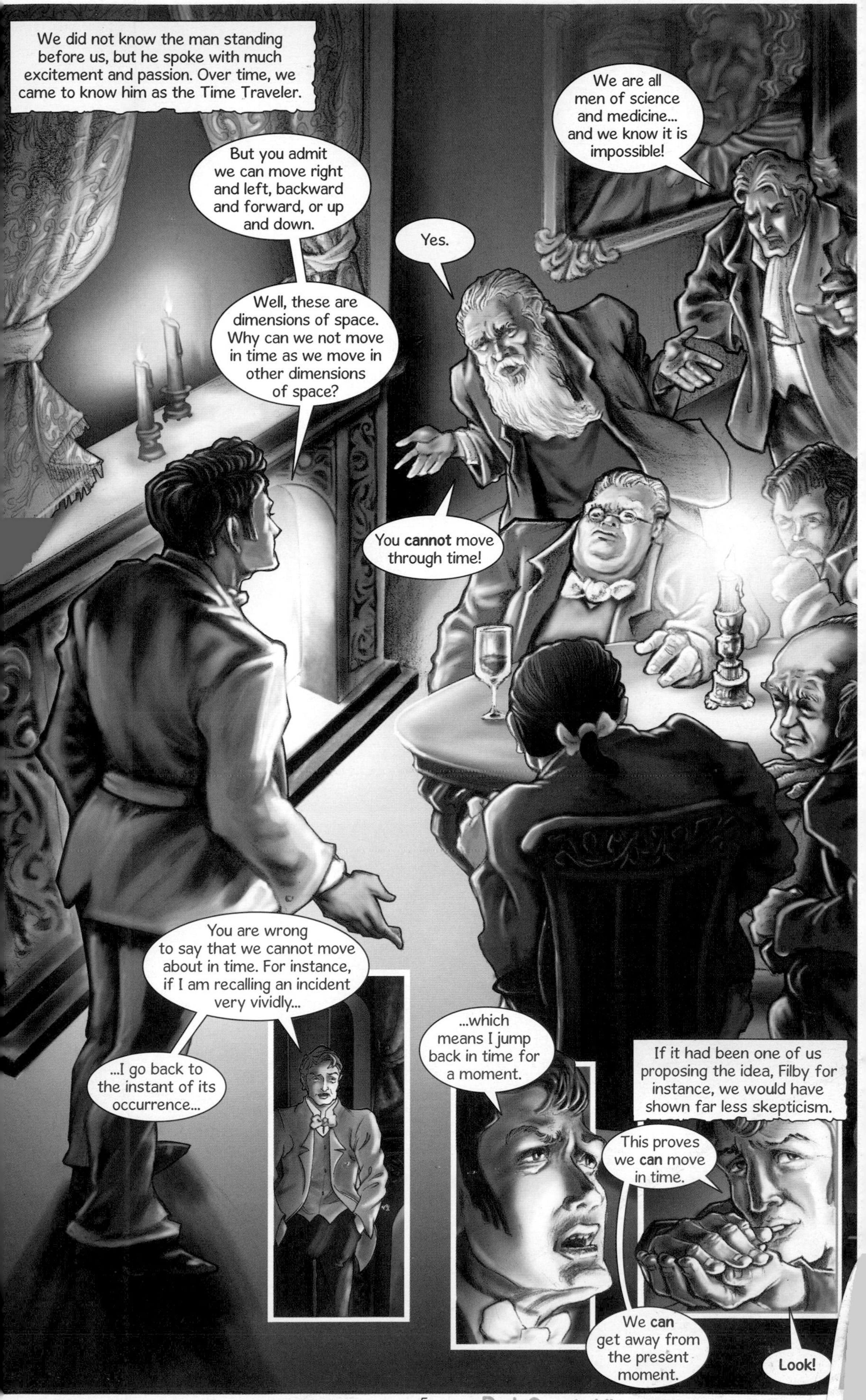

We did not know the man standing before us, but he spoke with much excitement and passion. Over time, we came to know him as the Time Traveler.
But you admit we can move right and left, backward and forward, or up and down.
Yes.
We are all men of science and medicine... and we know it is impossible!
Well, these are dimensions of space. Why can we not move in time as we move in other dimensions of space?
You **cannot** move through time!
You are wrong to say that we cannot move about in time. For instance, if I am recalling an incident very vividly...
...I go back to the instant of its occurrence...
...which means I jump back in time for a moment.
If it had been one of us proposing the idea, Filby for instance, we would have shown far less skepticism.
This proves we **can** move in time.
We **can** get away from the present moment.
Look!

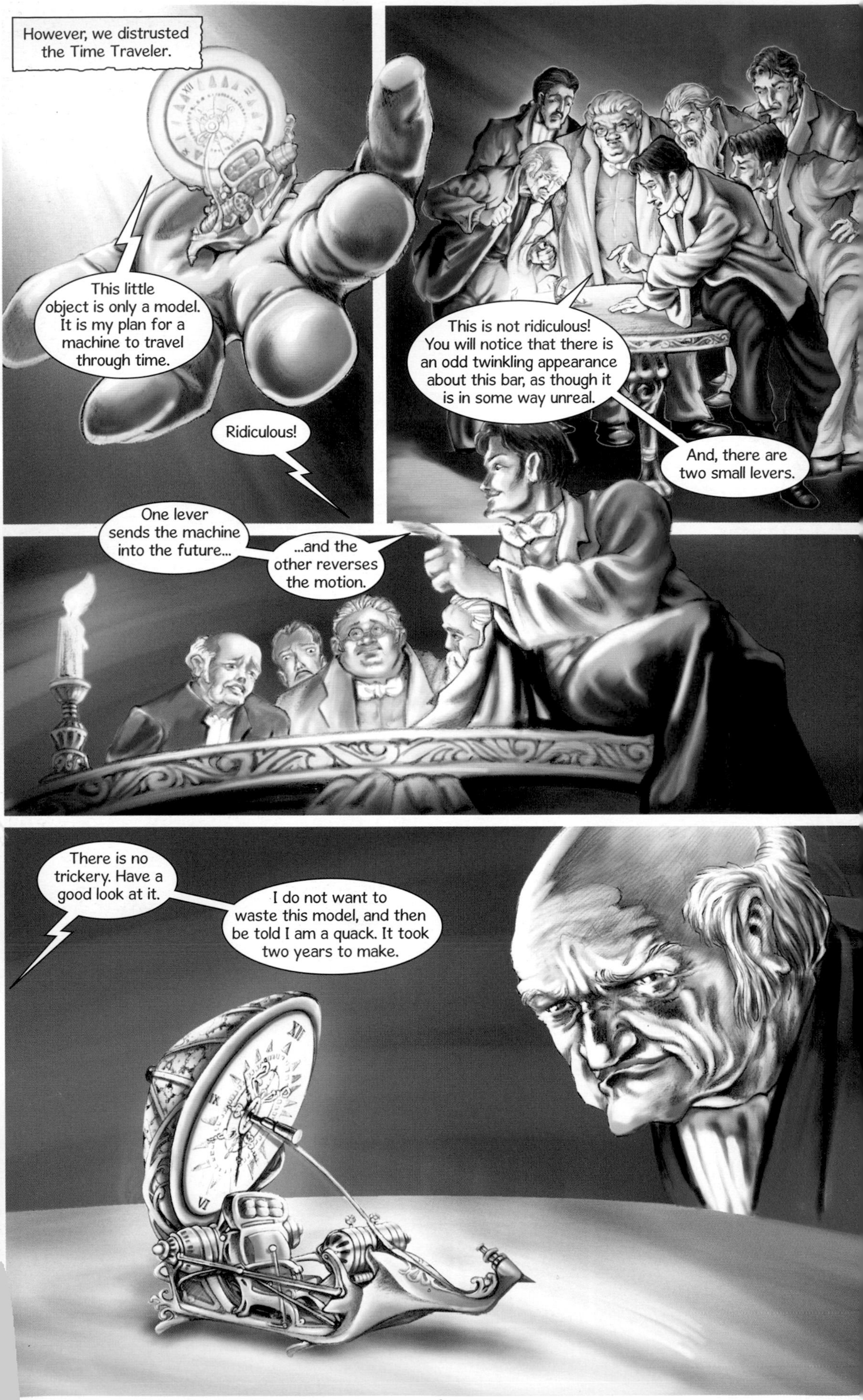
However, we distrusted the Time Traveler.
This little object is only a model. It is my plan for a machine to travel through time.
Ridiculous!
This is not ridiculous! You will notice that there is an odd twinkling appearance about this bar, as though it is in some way unreal.
And, there are two small levers.
One lever sends the machine into the future...
...and the other reverses the motion.
There is no trickery. Have a good look at it.
I do not want to waste this model, and then be told I am a quack. It took two years to make.

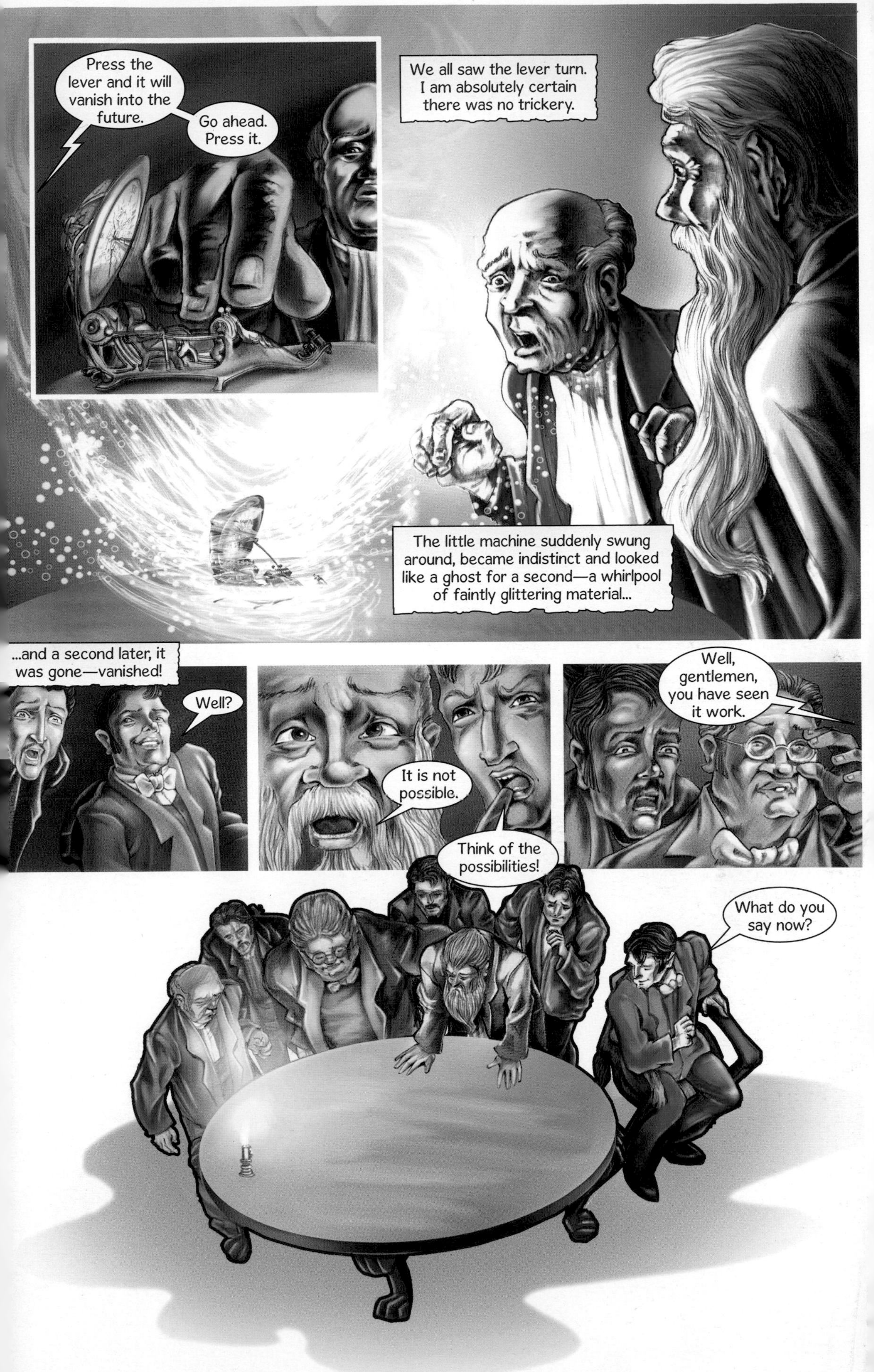
Press the lever and it will vanish into the future.
Go ahead. Press it.
We all saw the lever turn. I am absolutely certain there was no trickery.
The little machine suddenly swung around, became indistinct and looked like a ghost for a second—a whirlpool of faintly glittering material...
...and a second later, it was gone—vanished!
Well?
It is not possible.
Think of the possibilities!
Well, gentlemen, you have seen it work.
What do you say now?

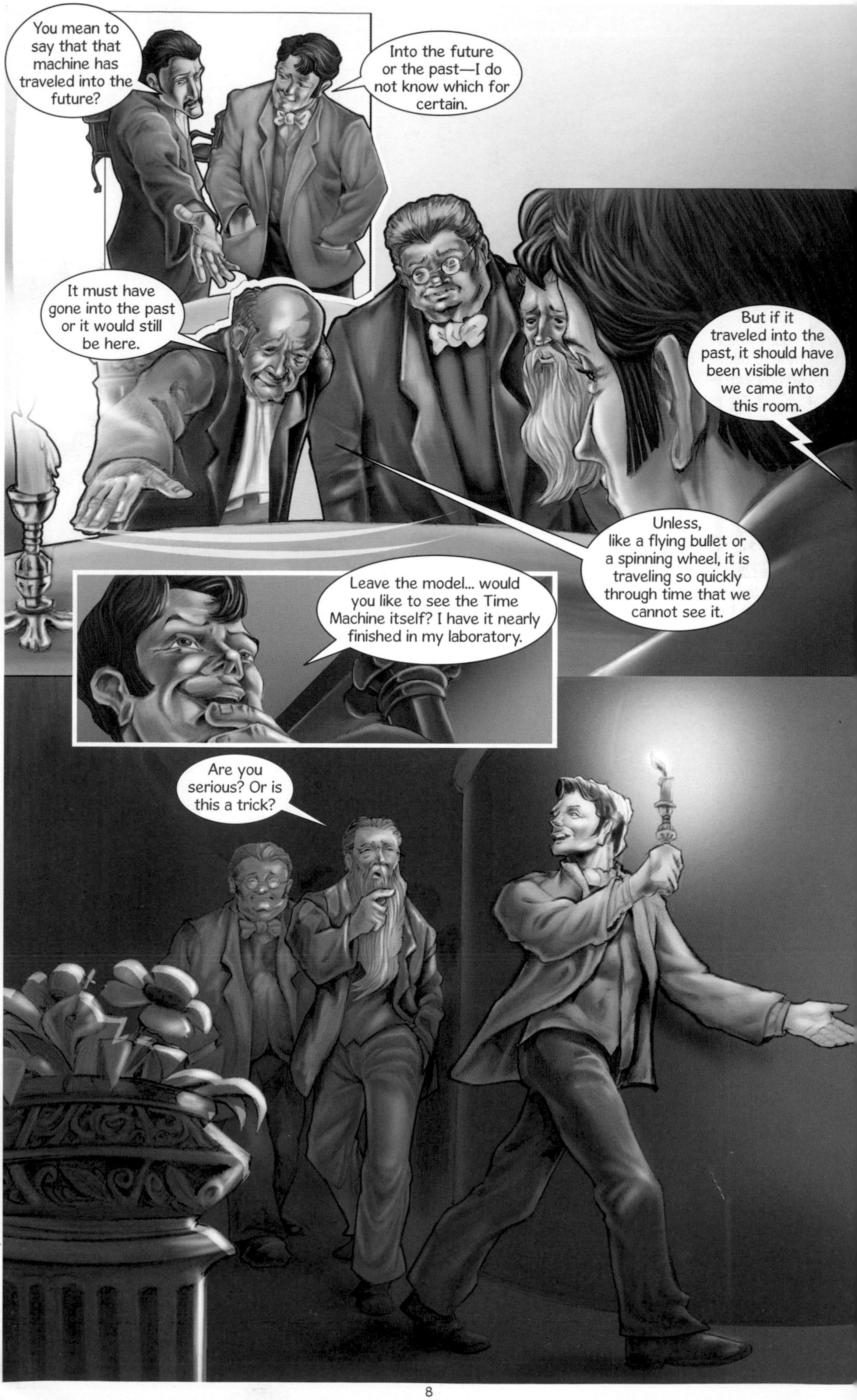

You mean to say that that machine has traveled into the future?
Into the future or the past—I do not know which for certain.
It must have gone into the past or it would still be here.
But if it traveled into the past, it should have been visible when we came into this room.
Unless, like a flying bullet or a spinning wheel, it is traveling so quickly through time that we cannot see it.
Leave the model... would you like to see the Time Machine itself? I have it nearly finished in my laboratory.
Are you serious? Or is this a trick?

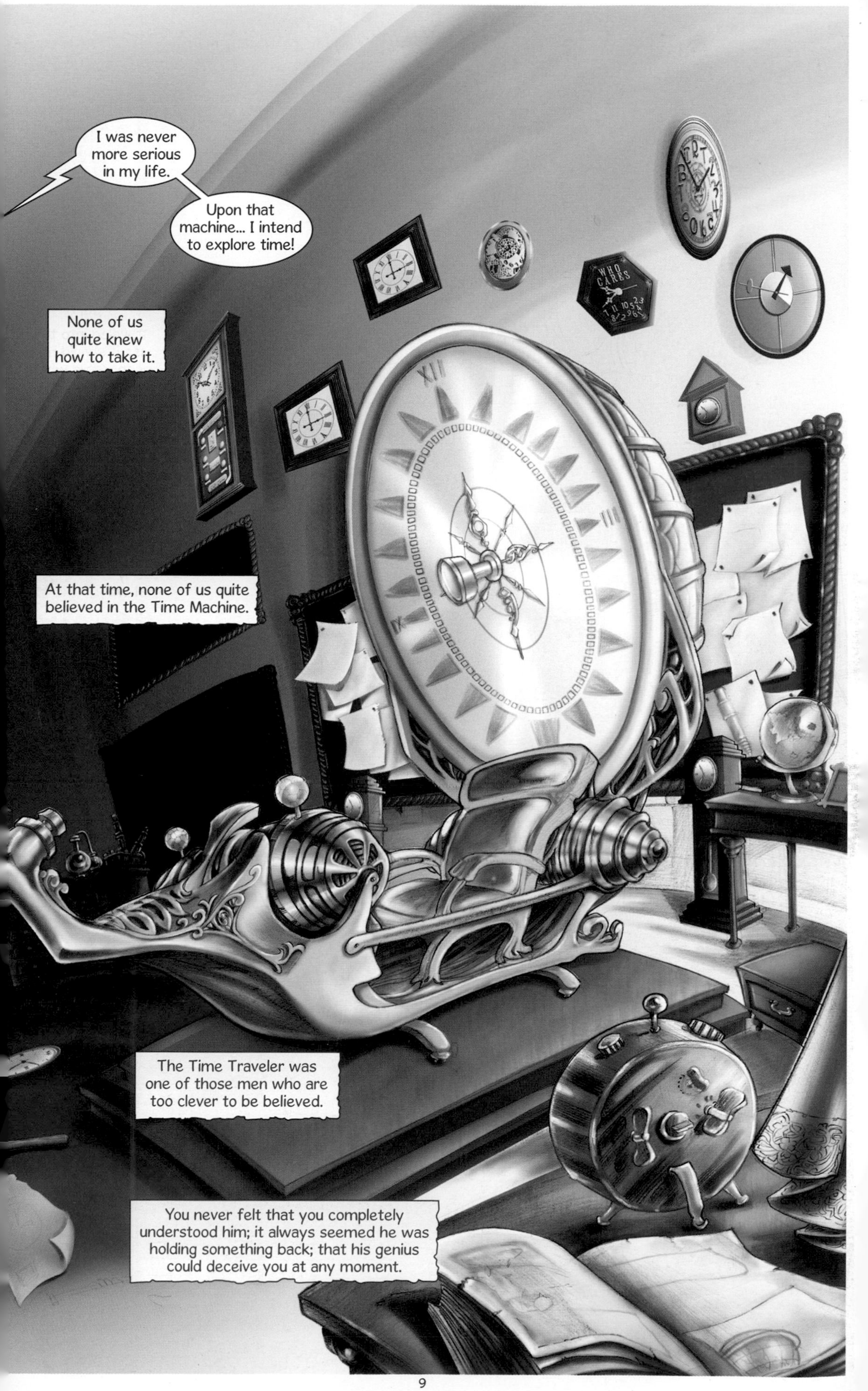
I was never more serious in my life.
Upon that machine... I intend to explore time!
None of us quite knew how to take it.
WHO CARES
At that time, none of us quite believed in the Time Machine.
The Time Traveler was one of those men who are too clever to be believed.
You never felt that you completely understood him; it always seemed he was holding something back; that his genius could deceive you at any moment.

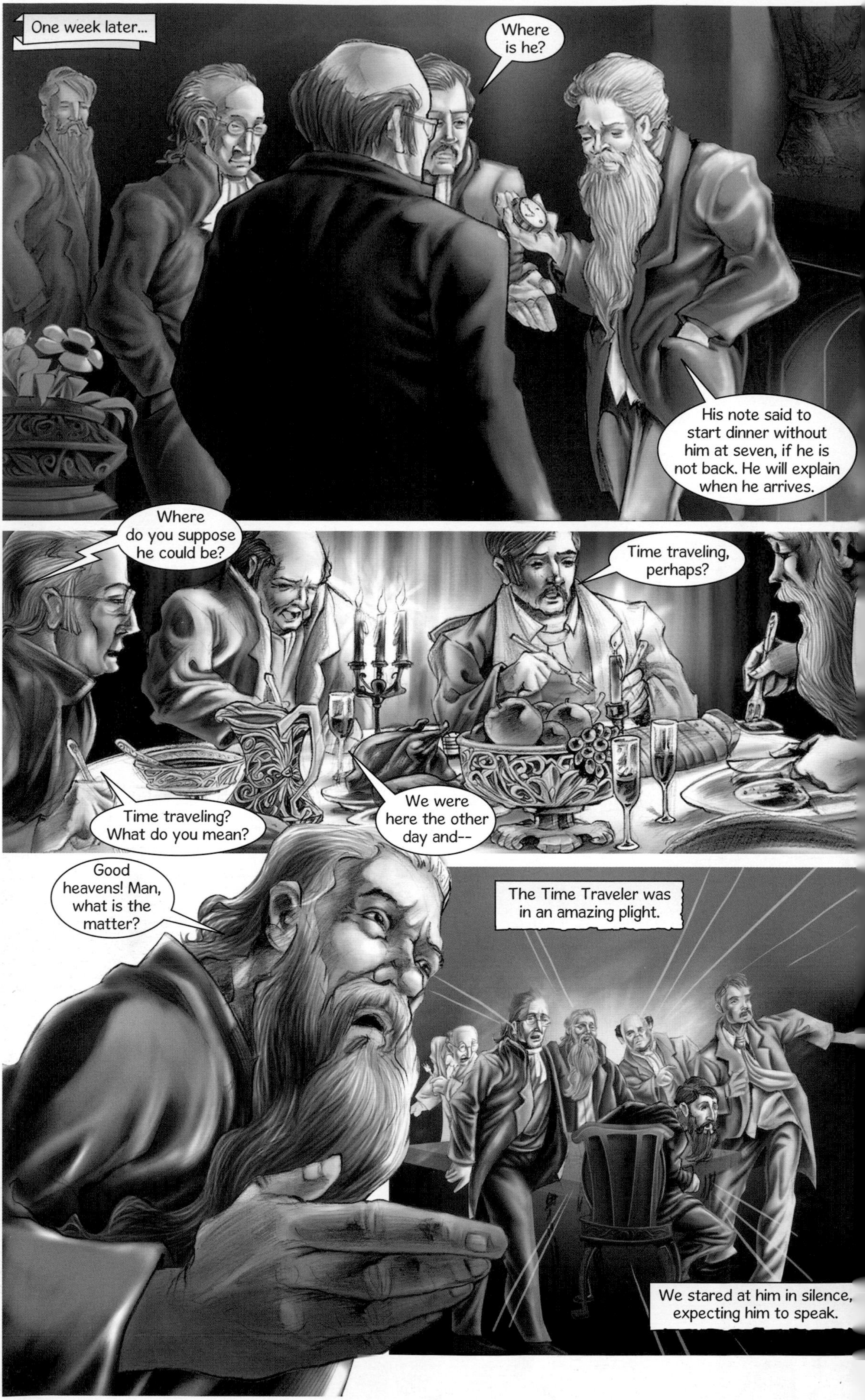
One week later...
Where is he?
His note said to start dinner without him at seven, if he is not back. He will explain when he arrives.
Where do you suppose he could be?
Time traveling, perhaps?
Time traveling? What do you mean?
We were here the other day and--
Good heavens! Man, what is the matter?
The Time Traveler was in an amazing plight.
We stared at him in silence, expecting him to speak.

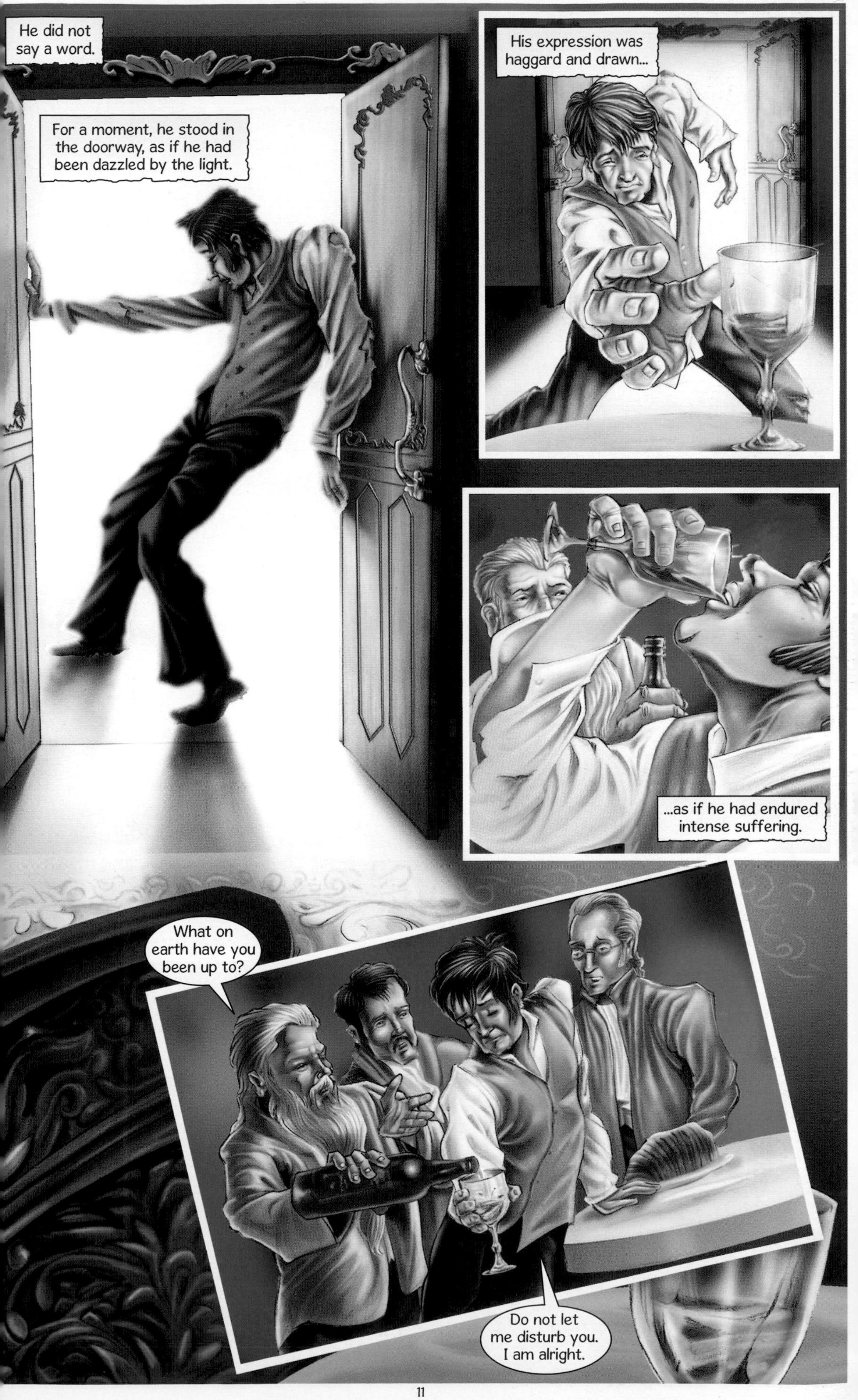

He did not say a word.
For a moment, he stood in the doorway, as if he had been dazzled by the light.
His expression was haggard and drawn...
...as if he had endured intense suffering.
What on earth have you been up to?
Do not let me disturb you. I am alright.

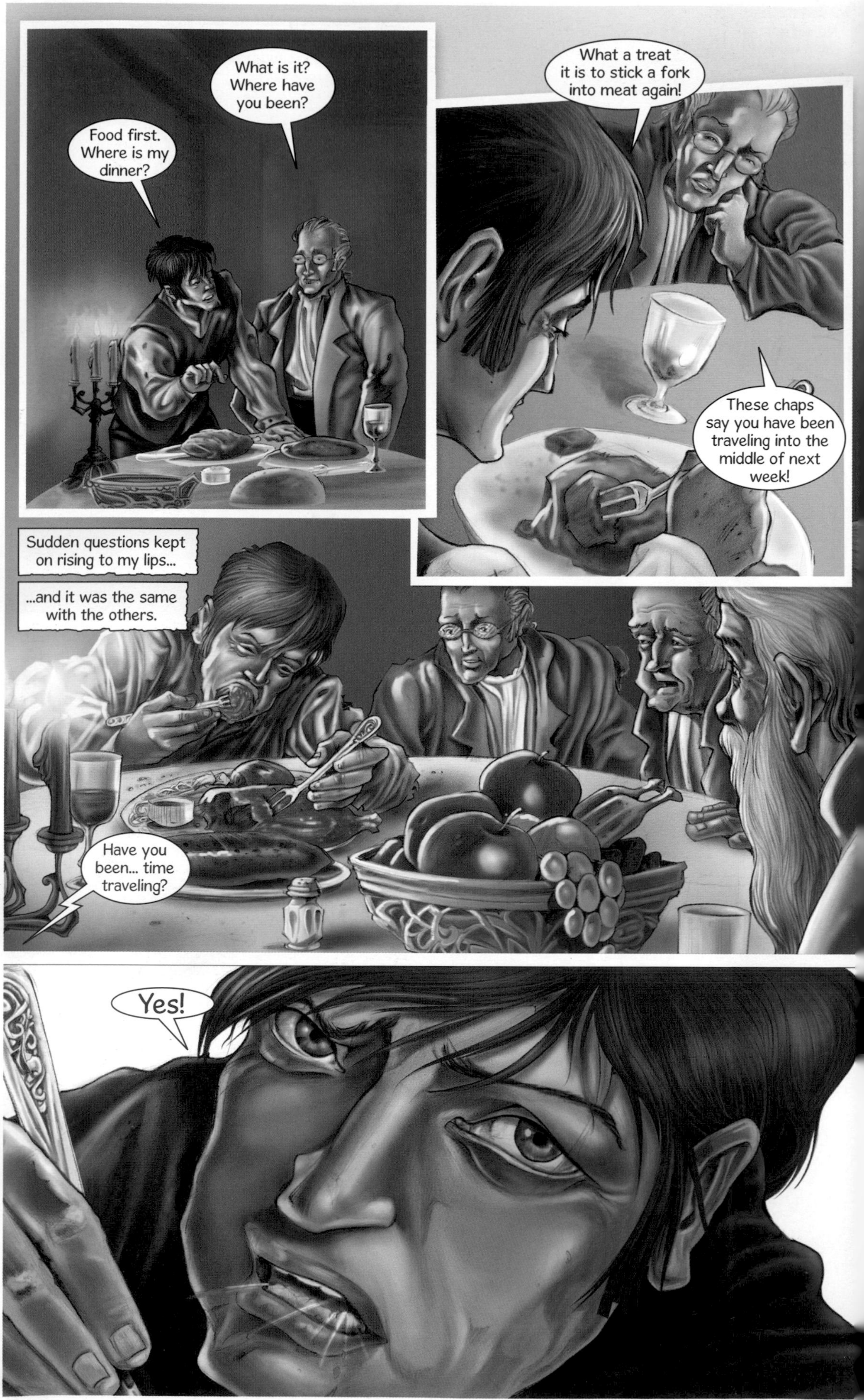
Food first. Where is my dinner?
What is it? Where have you been?
What a treat it is to stick a fork into meat again!
These chaps say you have been traveling into the middle of next week!
Sudden questions kept on rising to my lips...
...and it was the same with the others.
Have you been... time traveling?
Yes!

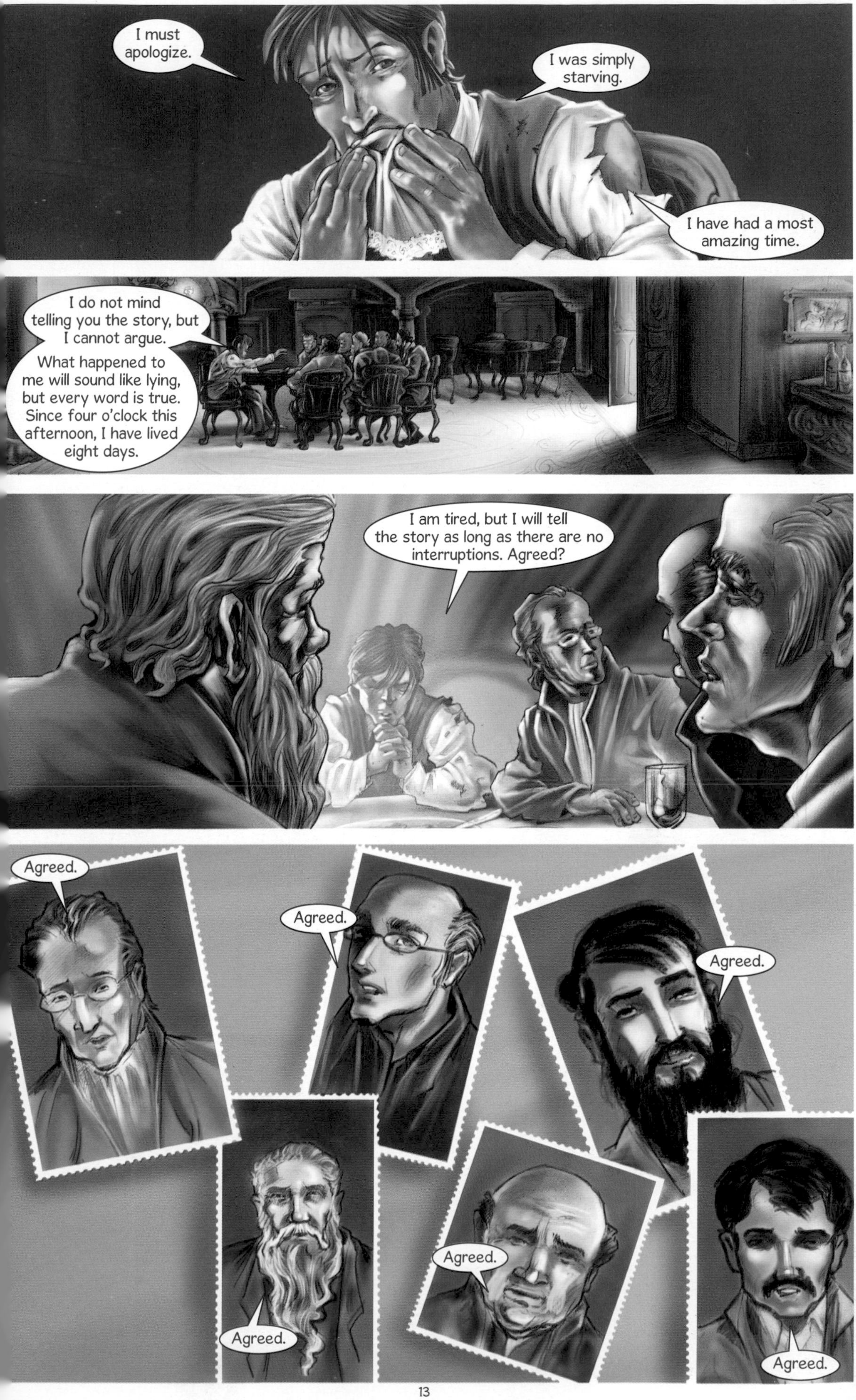
I must apologize.
I was simply starving.
I have had a most amazing time.
I do not mind telling you the story, but I cannot argue.
What happened to me will sound like lying, but every word is true. Since four o'clock this afternoon, I have lived eight days.
I am tired, but I will tell the story as long as there are no interruptions. Agreed?
Agreed.
Agreed.
Agreed.
Agreed.
Agreed.
Agreed.

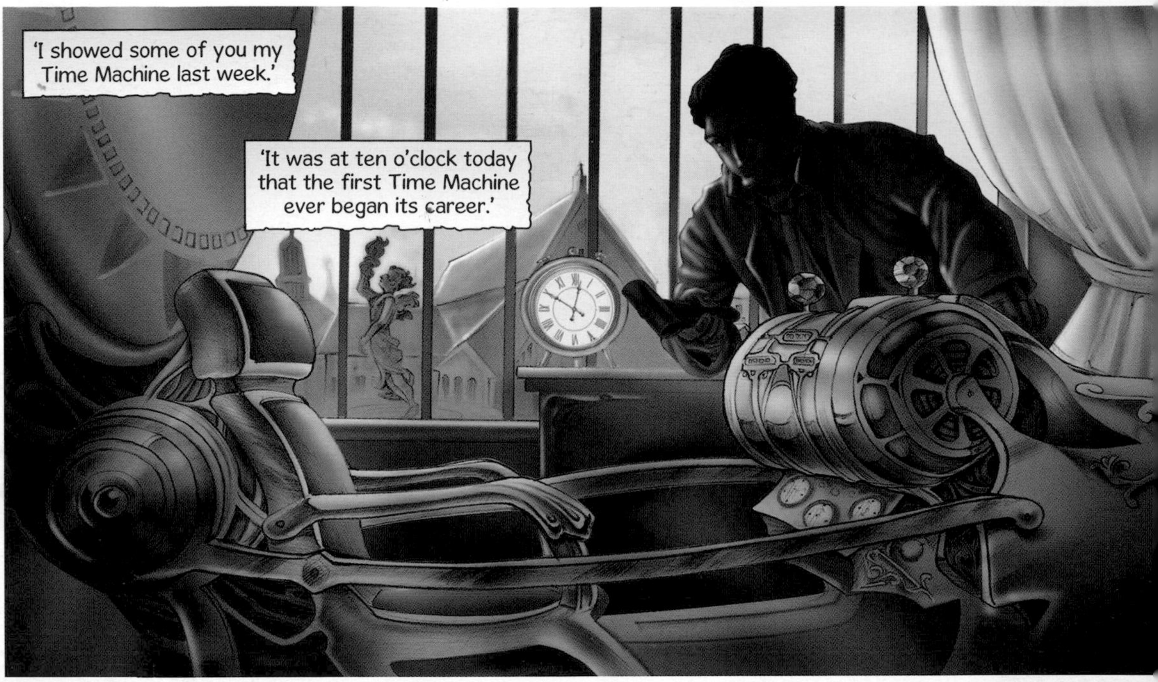
'I showed some of you my Time Machine last week.'
'It was at ten o'clock today that the first Time Machine ever began its career.'

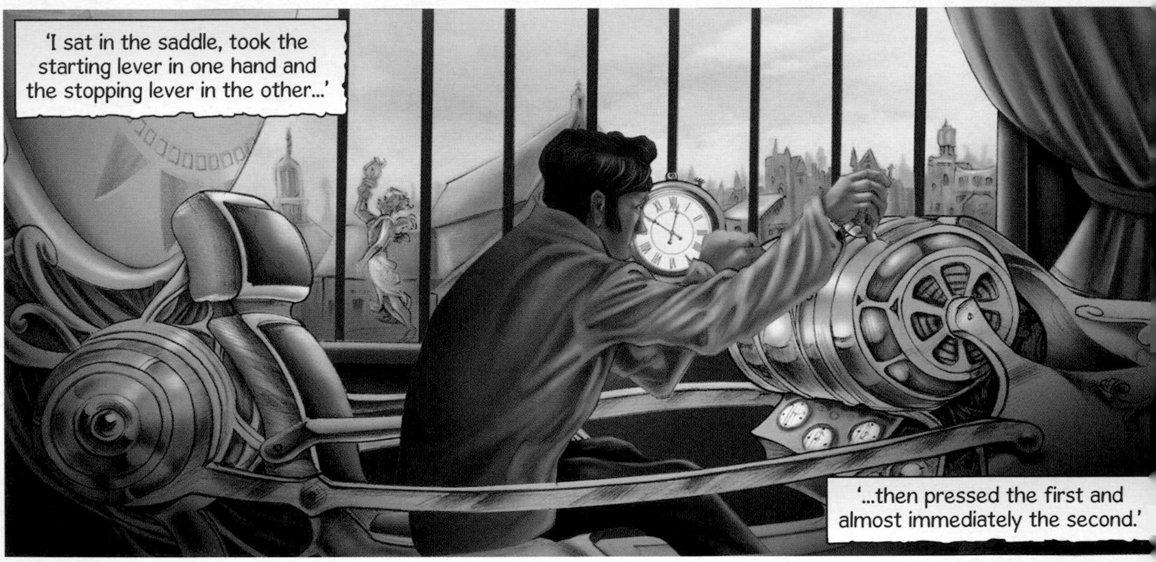
'I sat in the saddle, took the starting lever in one hand and the stopping lever in the other...'
'...then pressed the first and almost immediately the second.'

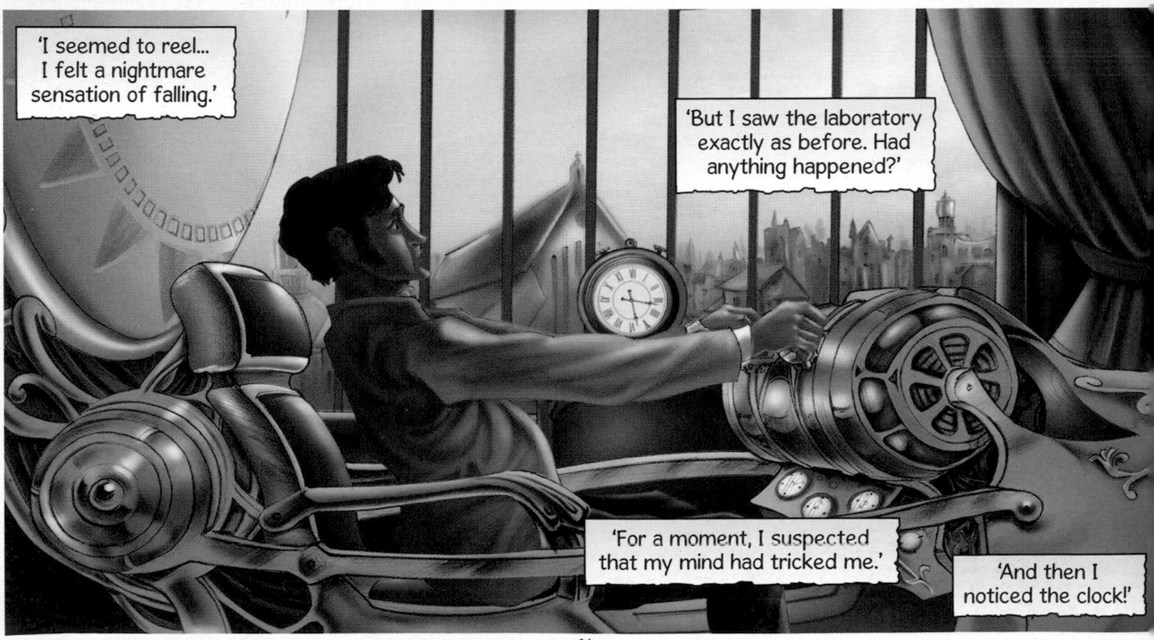
'I seemed to reel... I felt a nightmare sensation of falling.'
'But I saw the laboratory exactly as before. Had anything happened?'
'For a moment, I suspected that my mind had tricked me.'
'And then I noticed the clock!'

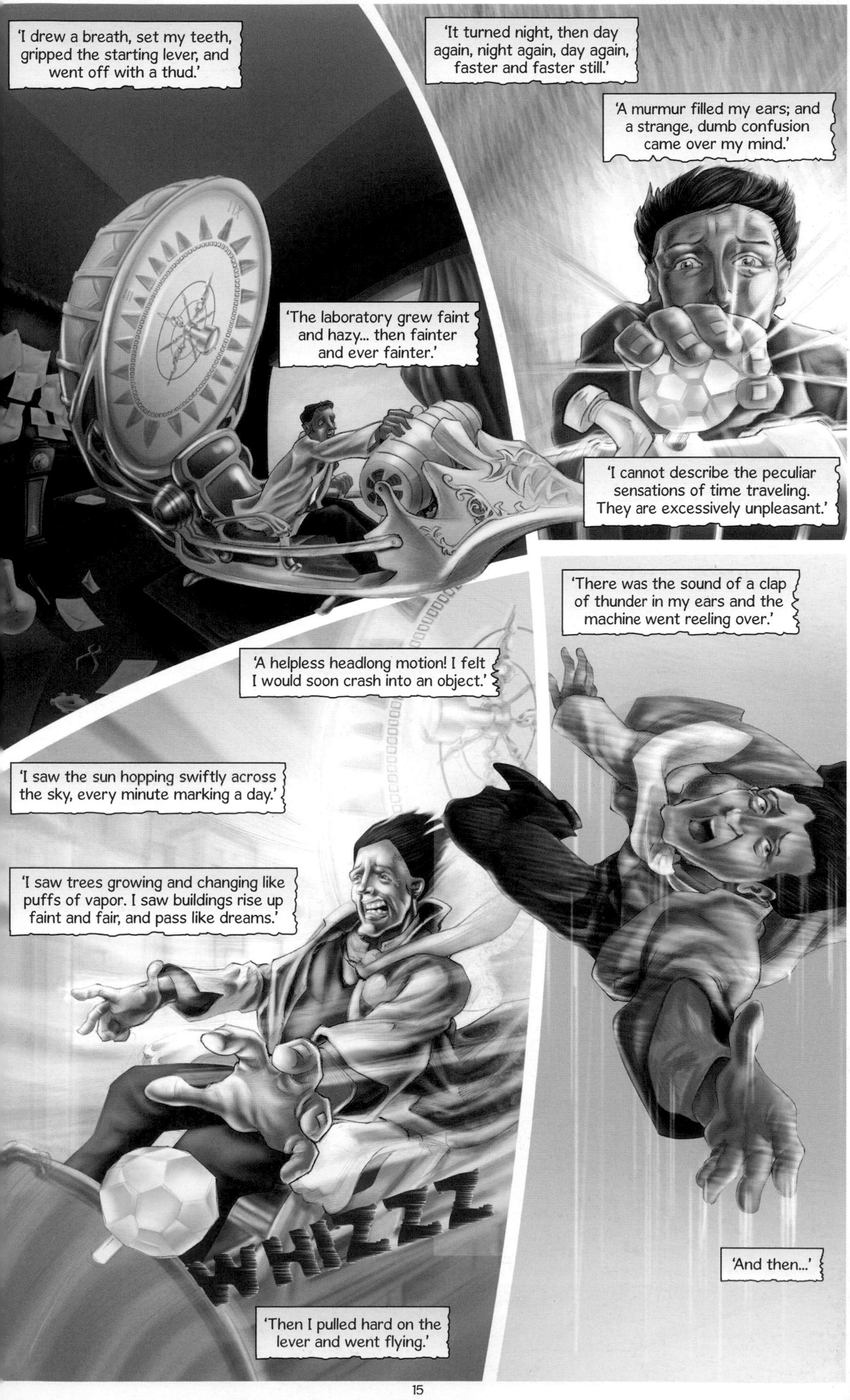
'I drew a breath, set my teeth, gripped the starting lever, and went off with a thud.'
'It turned night, then day again, night again, day again, faster and faster still.'
'A murmur filled my ears; and a strange, dumb confusion came over my mind.'
'The laboratory grew faint and hazy... then fainter and ever fainter.'
'I cannot describe the peculiar sensations of time traveling. They are excessively unpleasant.'
'There was the sound of a clap of thunder in my ears and the machine went reeling over.'
'A helpless headlong motion! I felt I would soon crash into an object.'
'I saw the sun hopping swiftly across the sky, every minute marking a day.'
'I saw trees growing and changing like puffs of vapor. I saw buildings rise up faint and fair, and pass like dreams.'
WHIZZZ
'Then I pulled hard on the lever and went flying.'
'And then...'

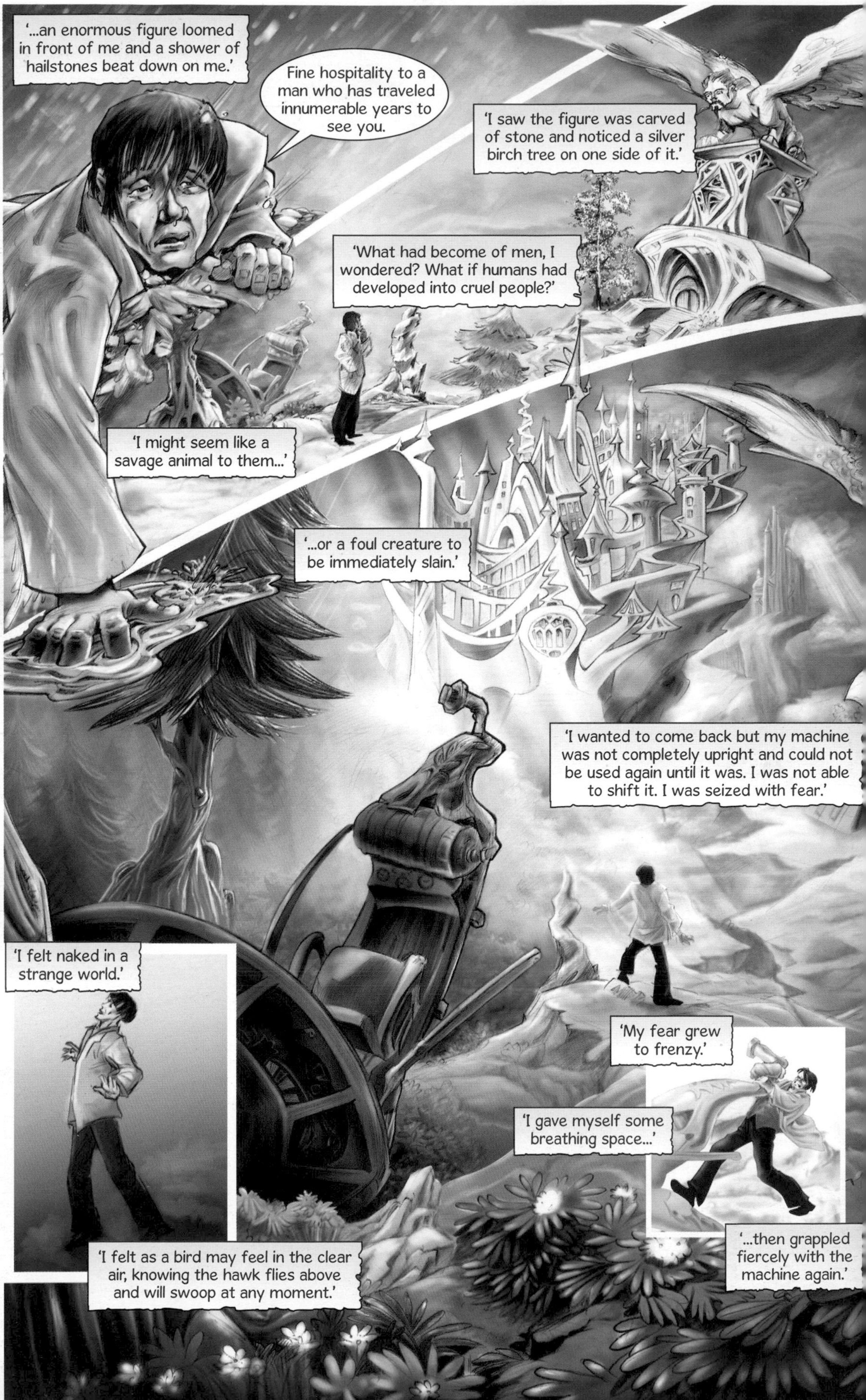
'...an enormous figure loomed in front of me and a shower of hailstones beat down on me.'
Fine hospitality to a man who has traveled innumerable years to see you.
'I saw the figure was carved of stone and noticed a silver birch tree on one side of it.'
'What had become of men, I wondered? What if humans had developed into cruel people?'
'I might seem like a savage animal to them...'
'...or a foul creature to be immediately slain.'
'I wanted to come back but my machine was not completely upright and could not be used again until it was. I was not able to shift it. I was seized with fear.'
'I felt naked in a strange world.'
'My fear grew to frenzy.'
'I gave myself some breathing space...'
'I felt as a bird may feel in the clear air, knowing the hawk flies above and will swoop at any moment.'
'...then grappled fiercely with the machine again.'

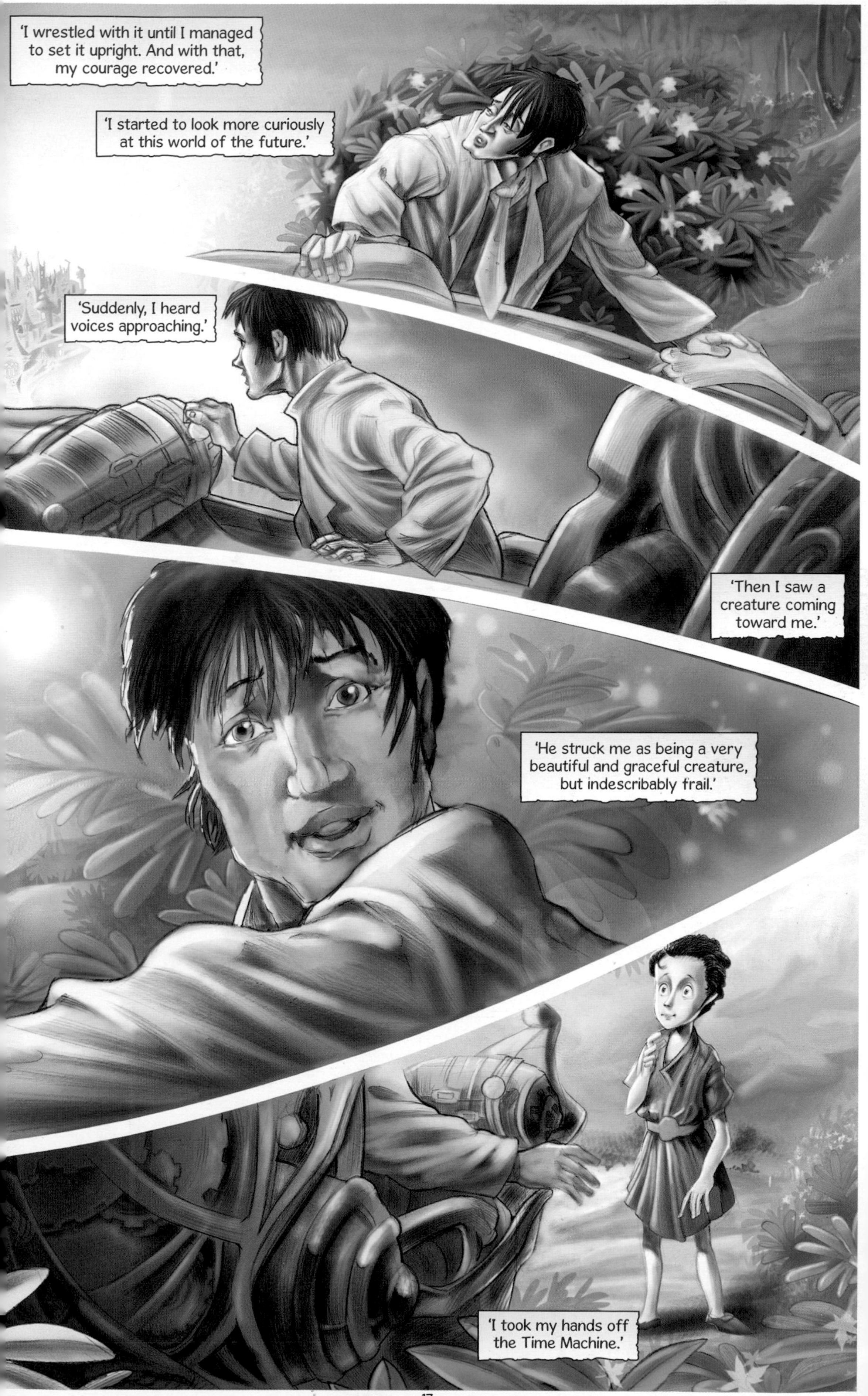
'I wrestled with it until I managed to set it upright. And with that, my courage recovered.'
'I started to look more curiously at this world of the future.'
'Suddenly, I heard voices approaching.'
'Then I saw a creature coming toward me.'
'He struck me as being a very beautiful and graceful creature, but indescribably frail.'
'I took my hands off the Time Machine.'

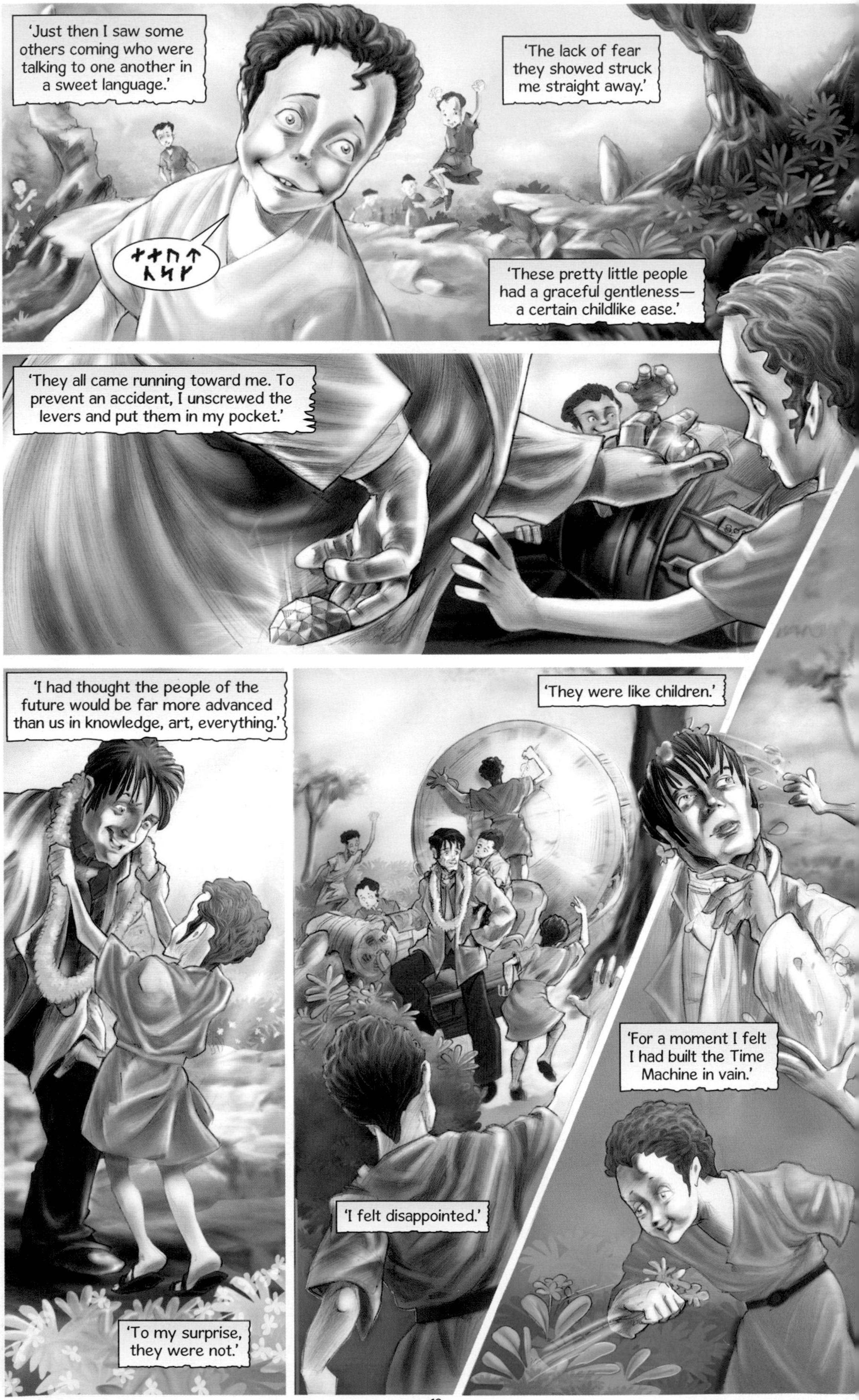
'Just then I saw some others coming who were talking to one another in a sweet language.'
'The lack of fear they showed struck me straight away.'
'These pretty little people had a graceful gentleness—a certain childlike ease.'
'They all came running toward me. To prevent an accident, I unscrewed the levers and put them in my pocket.'
'I had thought the people of the future would be far more advanced than us in knowledge, art, everything.'
'To my surprise, they were not.'
'They were like children.'
'I felt disappointed.'
'For a moment I felt I had built the Time Machine in vain.'

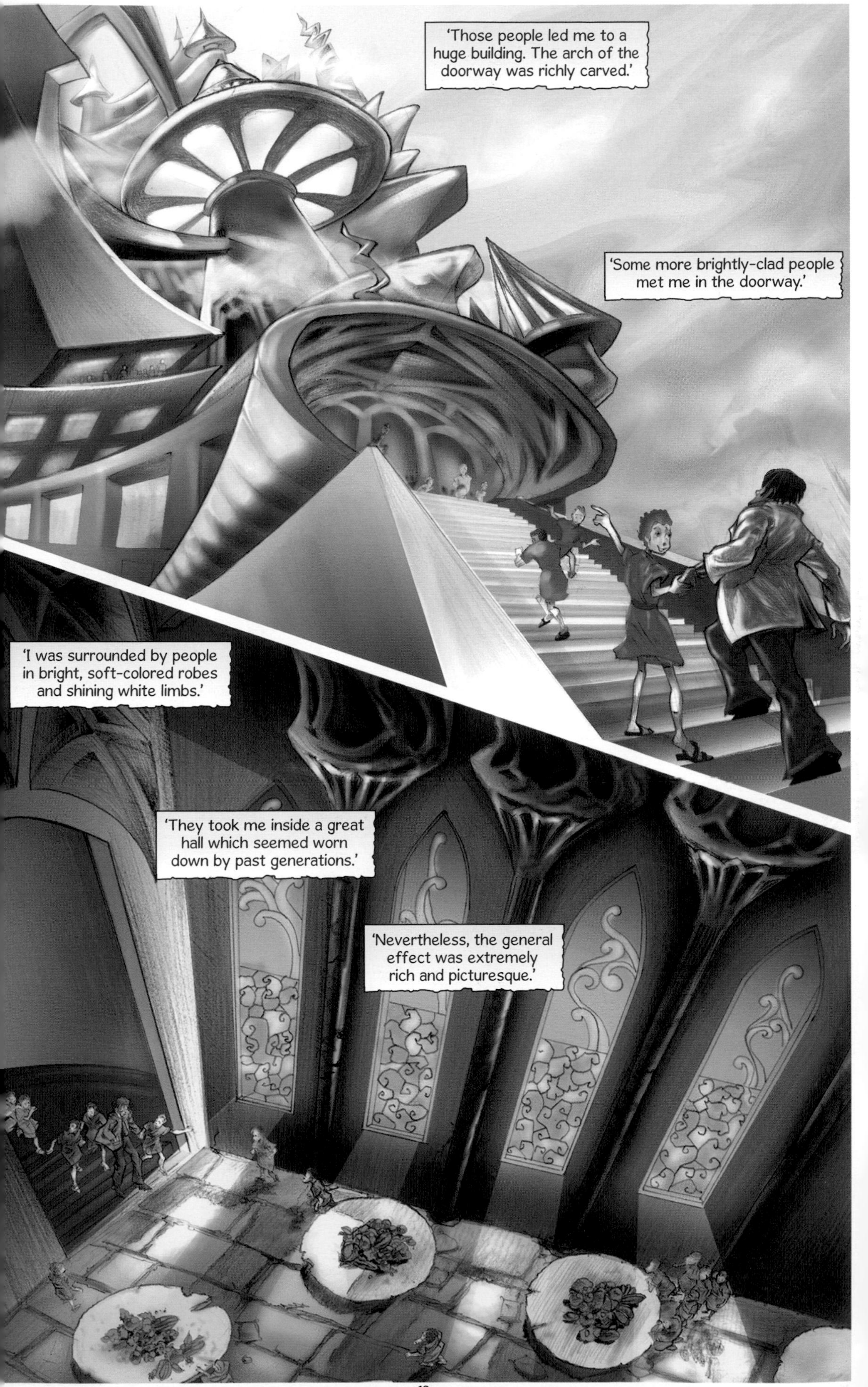
'Those people led me to a huge building. The arch of the doorway was richly carved.'
'Some more brightly-clad people met me in the doorway.'
'I was surrounded by people in bright, soft-colored robes and shining white limbs.'
'They took me inside a great hall which seemed worn down by past generations.'
'Nevertheless, the general effect was extremely rich and picturesque.'

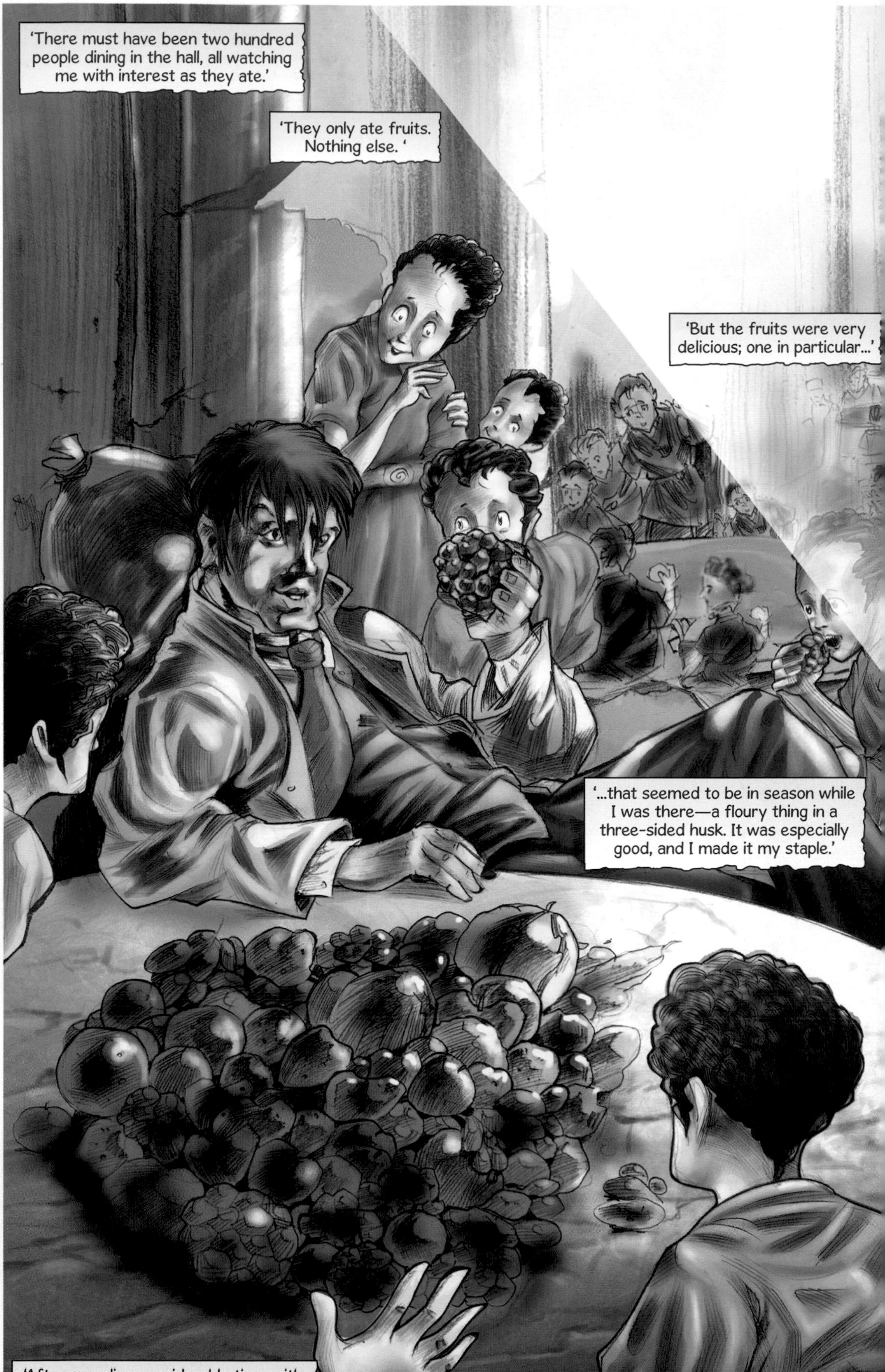
'There must have been two hundred people dining in the hall, all watching me with interest as they ate.'
'They only ate fruits. Nothing else. '
'But the fruits were very delicious; one in particular...'
'...that seemed to be in season while I was there—a floury thing in a three-sided husk. It was especially good, and I made it my staple.'
'After spending considerable time with them, I found out that horses, cattle, sheep and dogs were all extinct.'

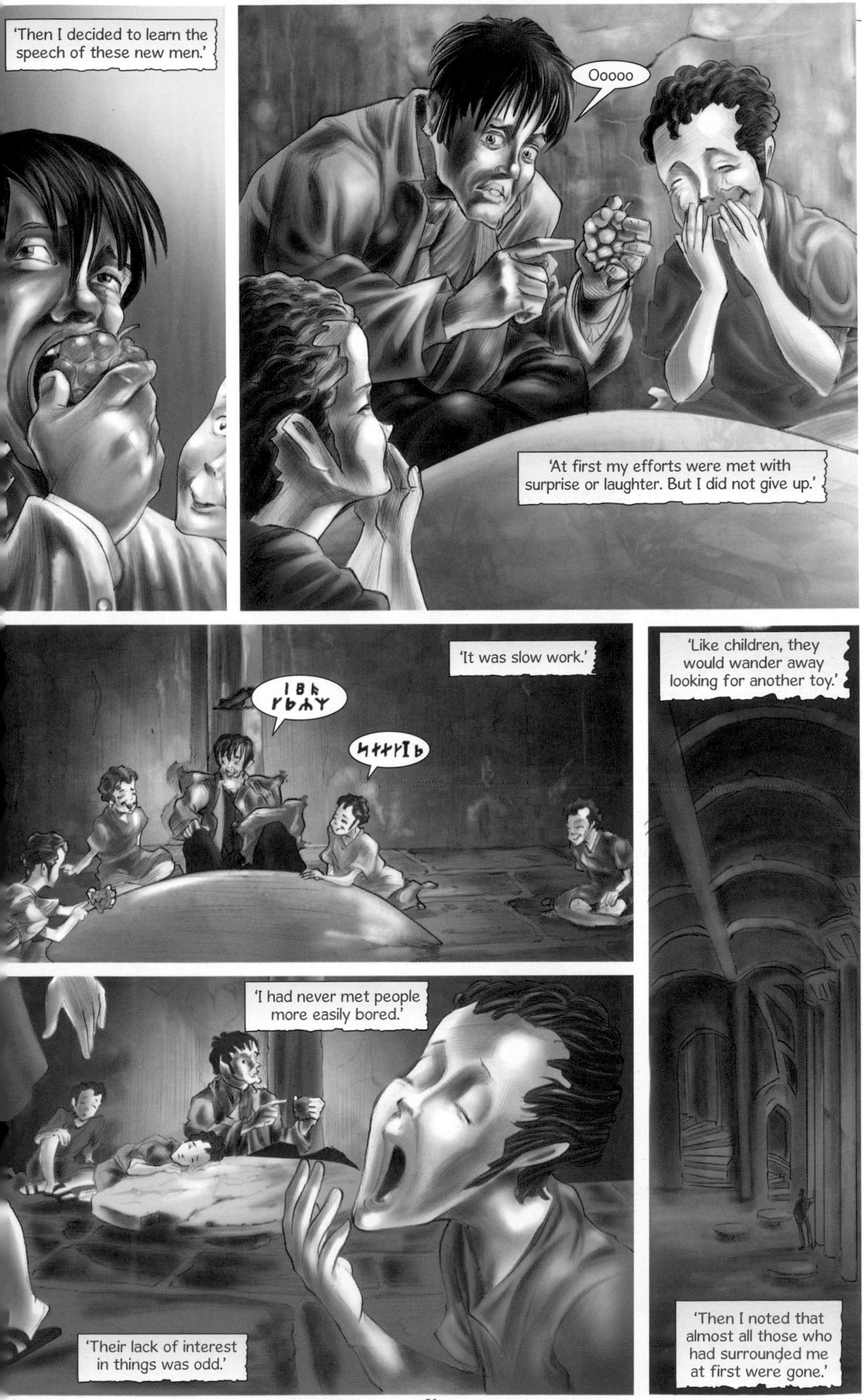
'Then I decided to learn the speech of these new men.'
Ooooo
'At first my efforts were met with surprise or laughter. But I did not give up.'
'It was slow work.'
'Like children, they would wander away looking for another toy.'
'I had never met people more easily bored.'
'Their lack of interest in things was odd.'
'Then I noted that almost all those who had surrounded me at first were gone.'

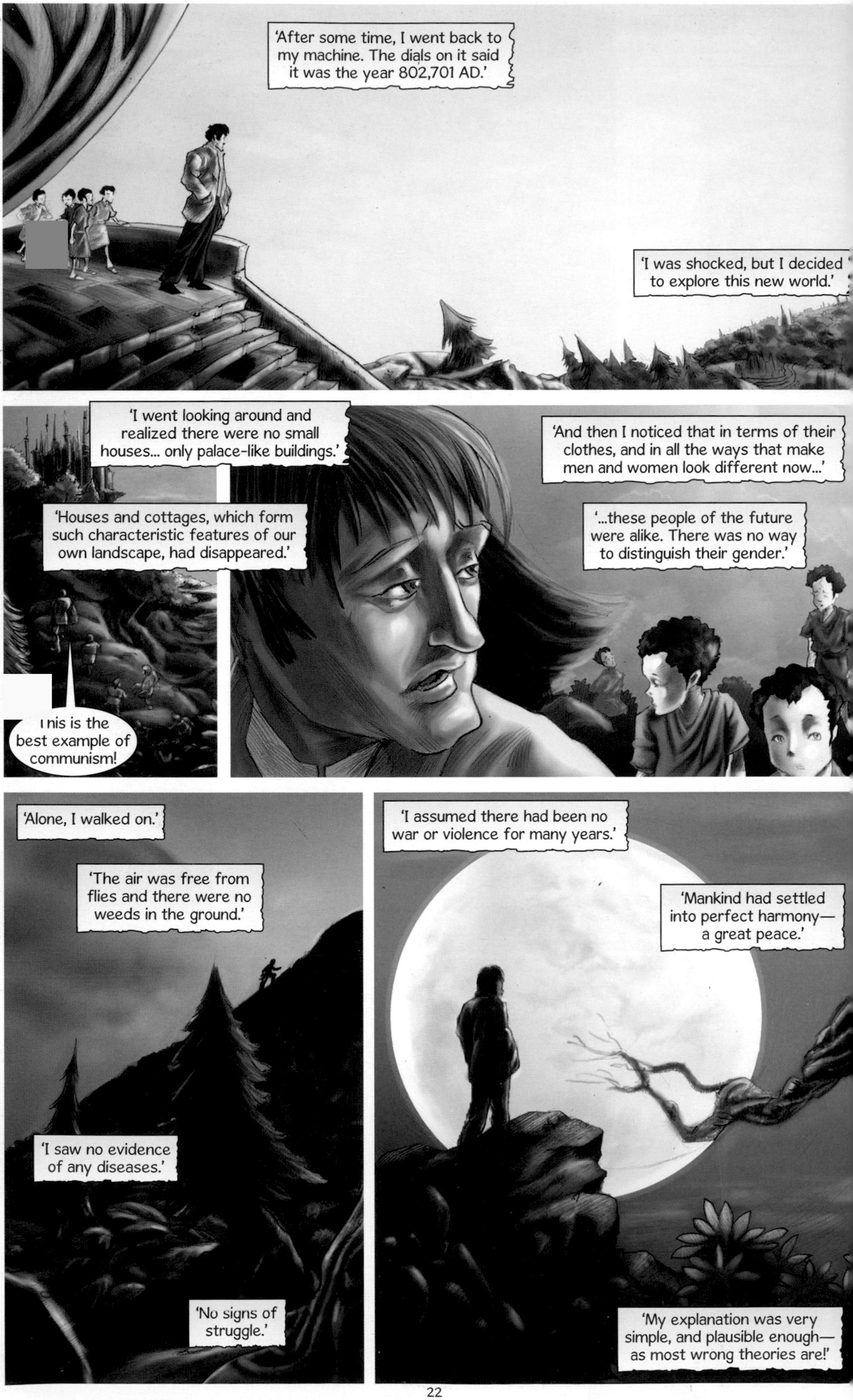
'After some time, I went back to my machine. The dials on it said it was the year 802,701 AD.'
'I was shocked, but I decided to explore this new world.'
'I went looking around and realized there were no small houses... only palace-like buildings.'
'Houses and cottages, which form such characteristic features of our own landscape, had disappeared.'
his is the best example of communism!
'And then I noticed that in terms of their clothes, and in all the ways that make men and women look different now...'
'...these people of the future were alike. There was no way to distinguish their gender.'
'Alone, I walked on.'
'The air was free from flies and there were no weeds in the ground.'
'I saw no evidence of any diseases.'
'No signs of struggle.'
'I assumed there had been no war or violence for many years.'
'Mankind had settled into perfect harmony— a great peace.'
'My explanation was very simple, and plausible enough— as most wrong theories are!'

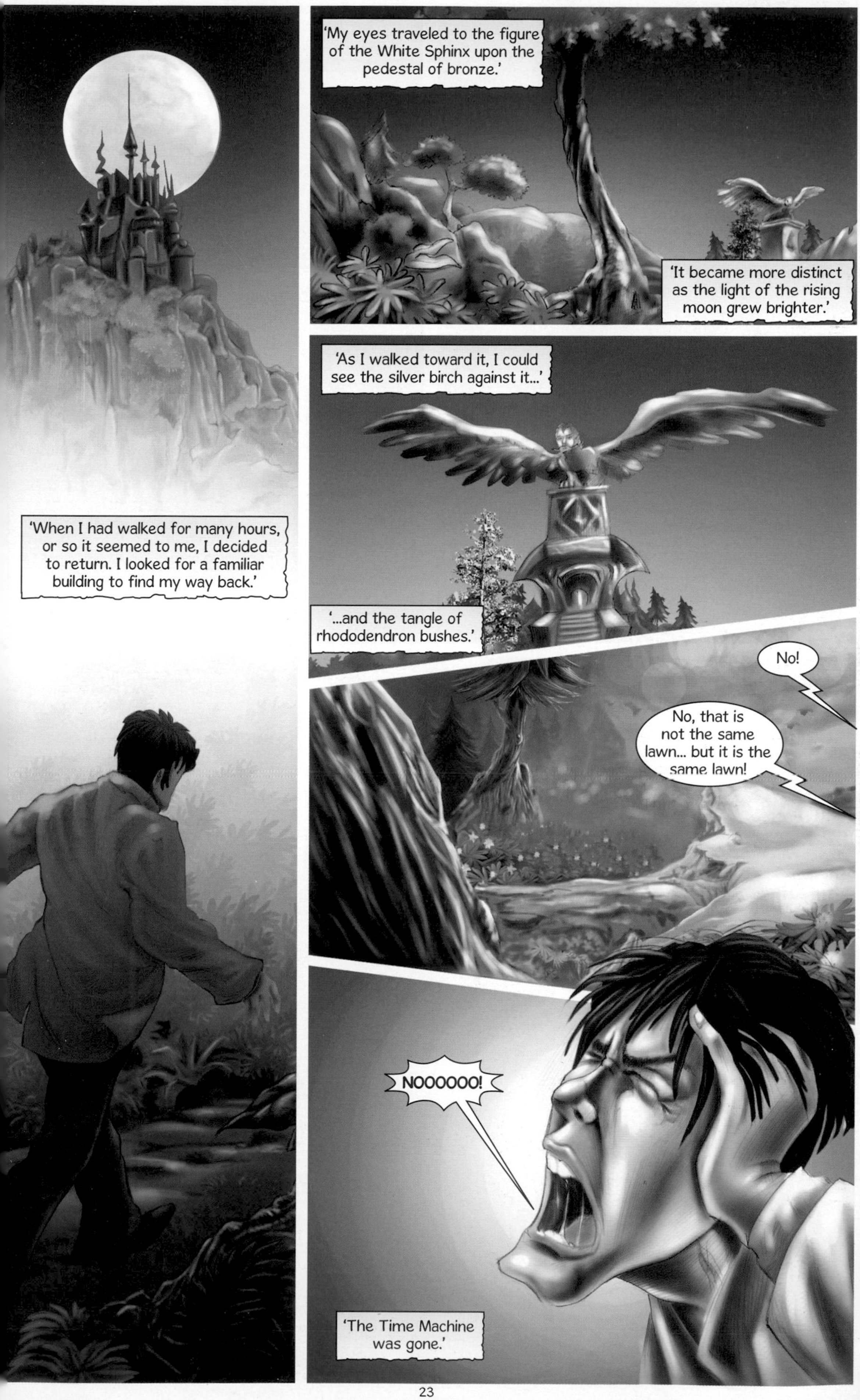

'When I had walked for many hours, or so it seemed to me, I decided to return. I looked for a familiar building to find my way back.'
'My eyes traveled to the figure of the White Sphinx upon the pedestal of bronze.'
'It became more distinct as the light of the rising moon grew brighter.'
'As I walked toward it, I could see the silver birch against it...'
'...and the tangle of rhododendron bushes.'
No!
No, that is not the same lawn... but it is the same lawn!
NOOOOOO!
'The Time Machine was gone.'

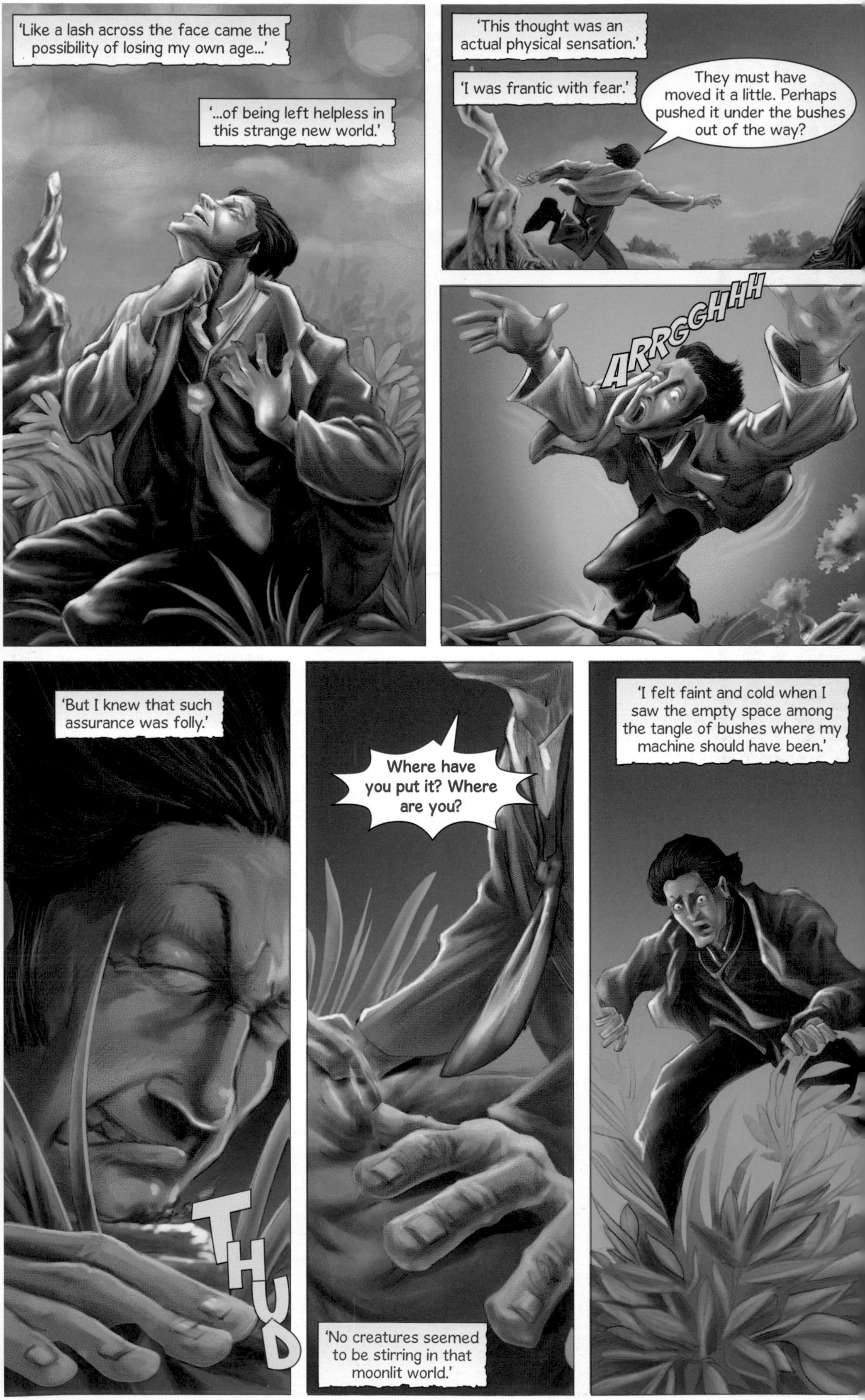

'Like a lash across the face came the possibility of losing my own age...'
'...of being left helpless in this strange new world.'
'This thought was an actual physical sensation.'
'I was frantic with fear.'
They must have moved it a little. Perhaps pushed it under the bushes out of the way?
ARRGGHHH
'But I knew that such assurance was folly.'
THUD
Where have you put it? Where are you?
'No creatures seemed to be stirring in that moonlit world.'
'I felt faint and cold when I saw the empty space among the tangle of bushes where my machine should have been.'

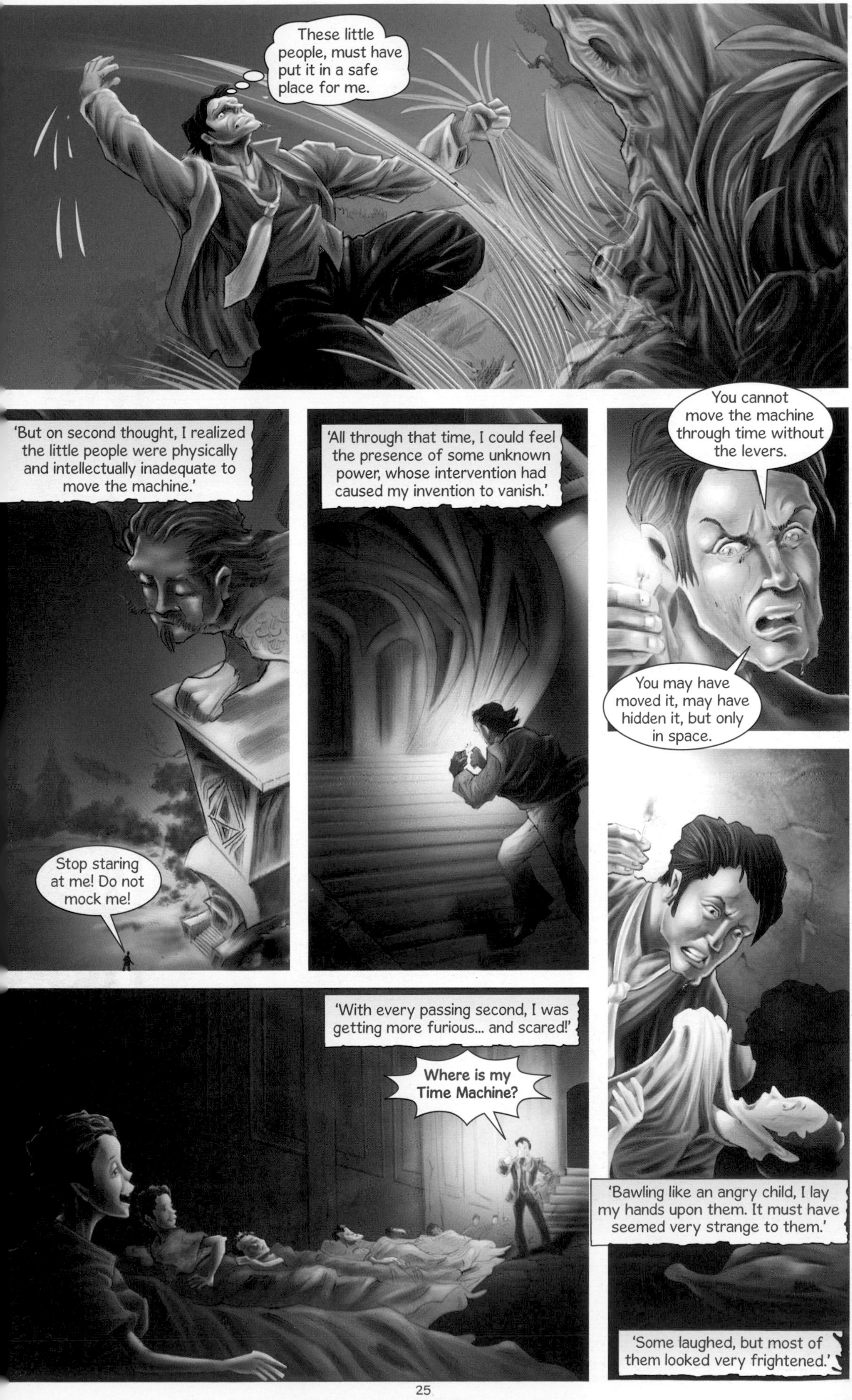
These little people, must have put it in a safe place for me.
'But on second thought, I realized the little people were physically and intellectually inadequate to move the machine.'
Stop staring at me! Do not mock me!
'All through that time, I could feel the presence of some unknown power, whose intervention had caused my invention to vanish.'
You cannot move the machine through time without the levers.
You may have moved it, may have hidden it, but only in space.
'With every passing second, I was getting more furious... and scared!'
Where is my Time Machine?
'Bawling like an angry child, I lay my hands upon them. It must have seemed very strange to them.'
'Some laughed, but most of them looked very frightened.'

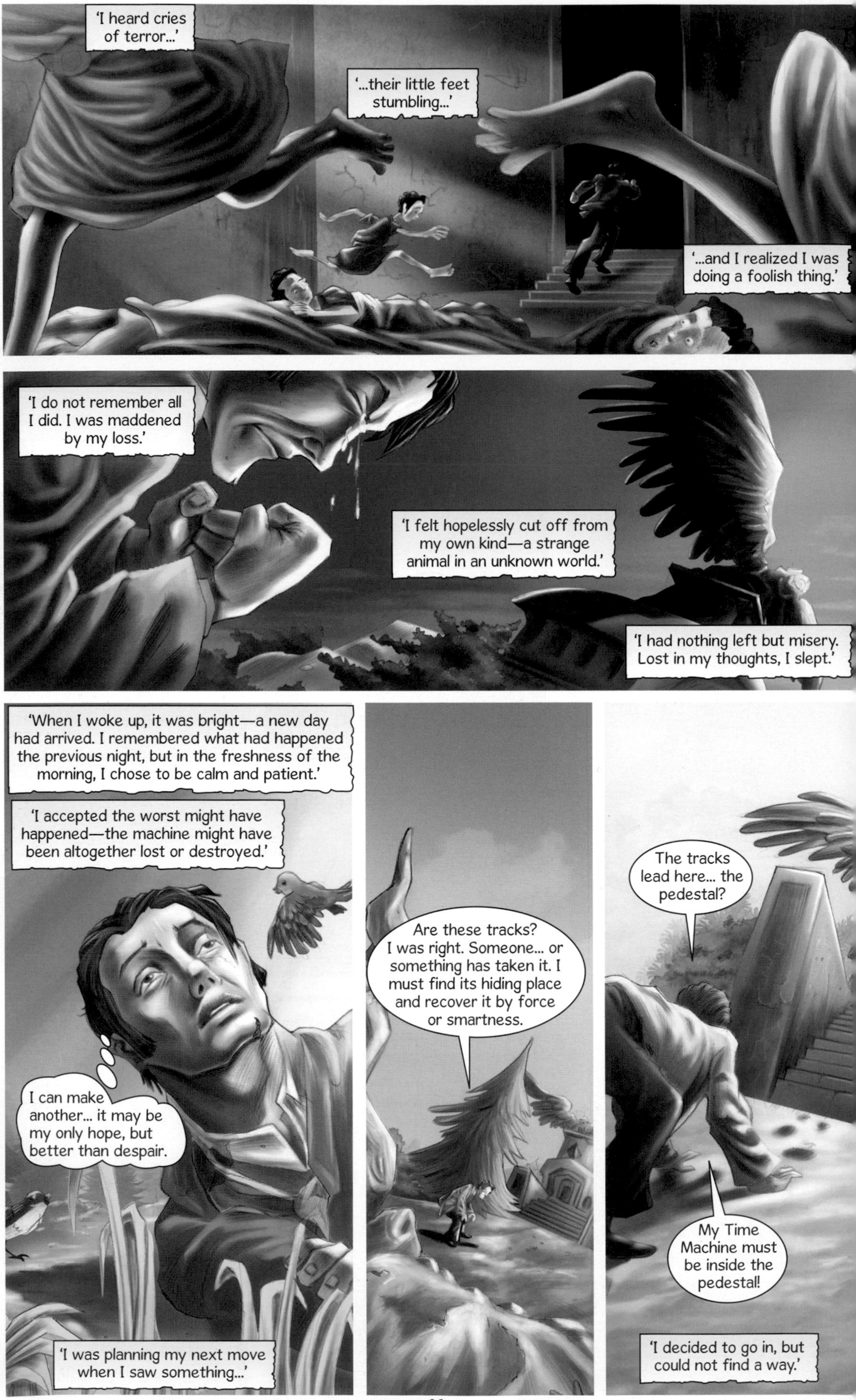
'I heard cries of terror...'
'...their little feet stumbling...'
'...and I realized I was doing a foolish thing.'
'I do not remember all I did. I was maddened by my loss.'
'I felt hopelessly cut off from my own kind—a strange animal in an unknown world.'
'I had nothing left but misery. Lost in my thoughts, I slept.'
'When I woke up, it was bright—a new day had arrived. I remembered what had happened the previous night, but in the freshness of the morning, I chose to be calm and patient.'
'I accepted the worst might have happened—the machine might have been altogether lost or destroyed.'
I can make another... it may be my only hope, but better than despair.
'I was planning my next move when I saw something...'
Are these tracks? I was right. Someone... or something has taken it. I must find its hiding place and recover it by force or smartness.
The tracks lead here... the pedestal?
My Time Machine must be inside the pedestal!
'I decided to go in, but could not find a way.'

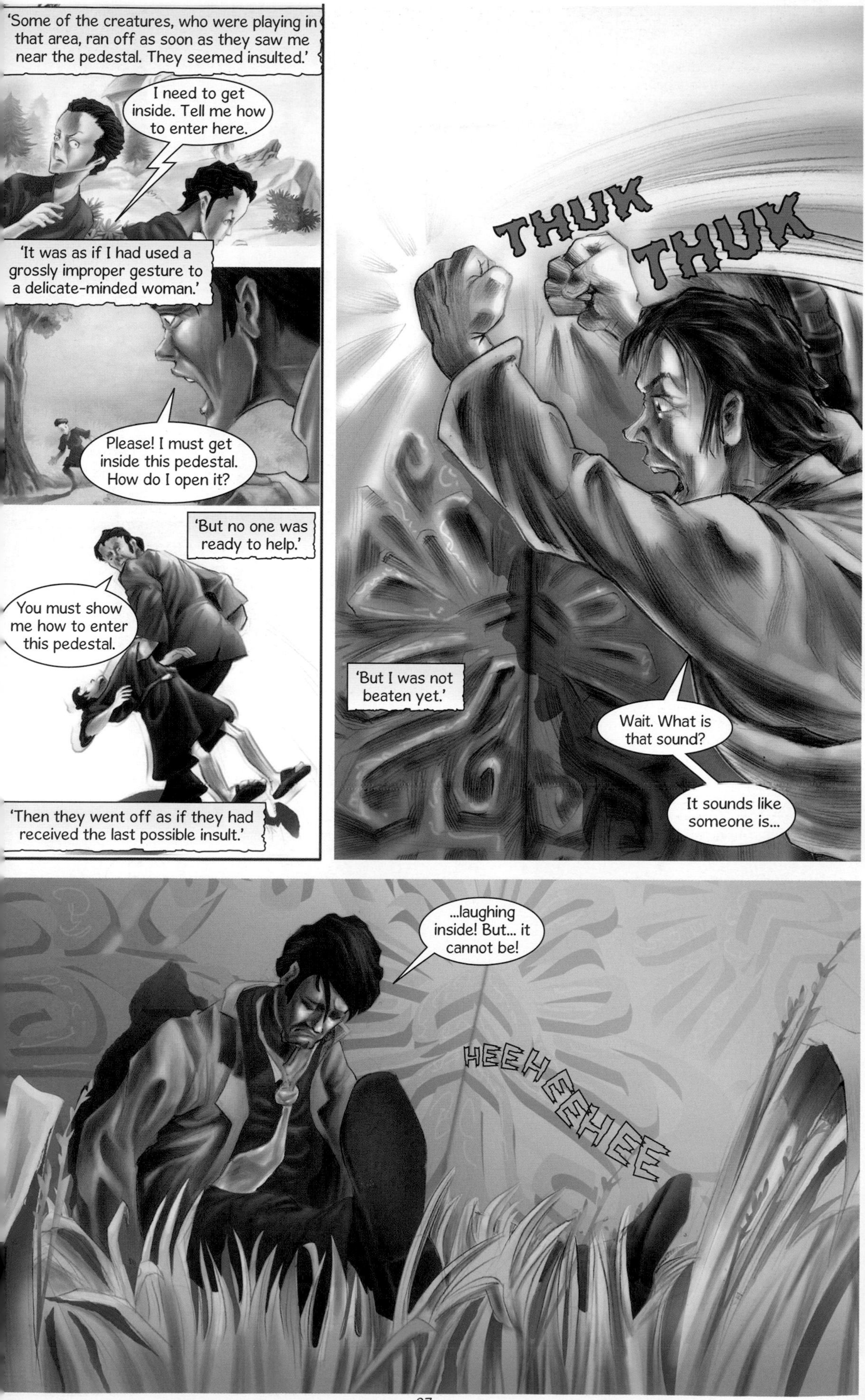
'Some of the creatures, who were playing in that area, ran off as soon as they saw me near the pedestal. They seemed insulted.'
I need to get inside. Tell me how to enter here.
'It was as if I had used a grossly improper gesture to a delicate-minded woman.'
Please! I must get inside this pedestal. How do I open it?
'But no one was ready to help.'
You must show me how to enter this pedestal.
'Then they went off as if they had received the last possible insult.'
THUK THUK
'But I was not beaten yet.'
Wait. What is that sound?
It sounds like someone is...
...laughing inside! But... it cannot be!
HEEHEEHEE

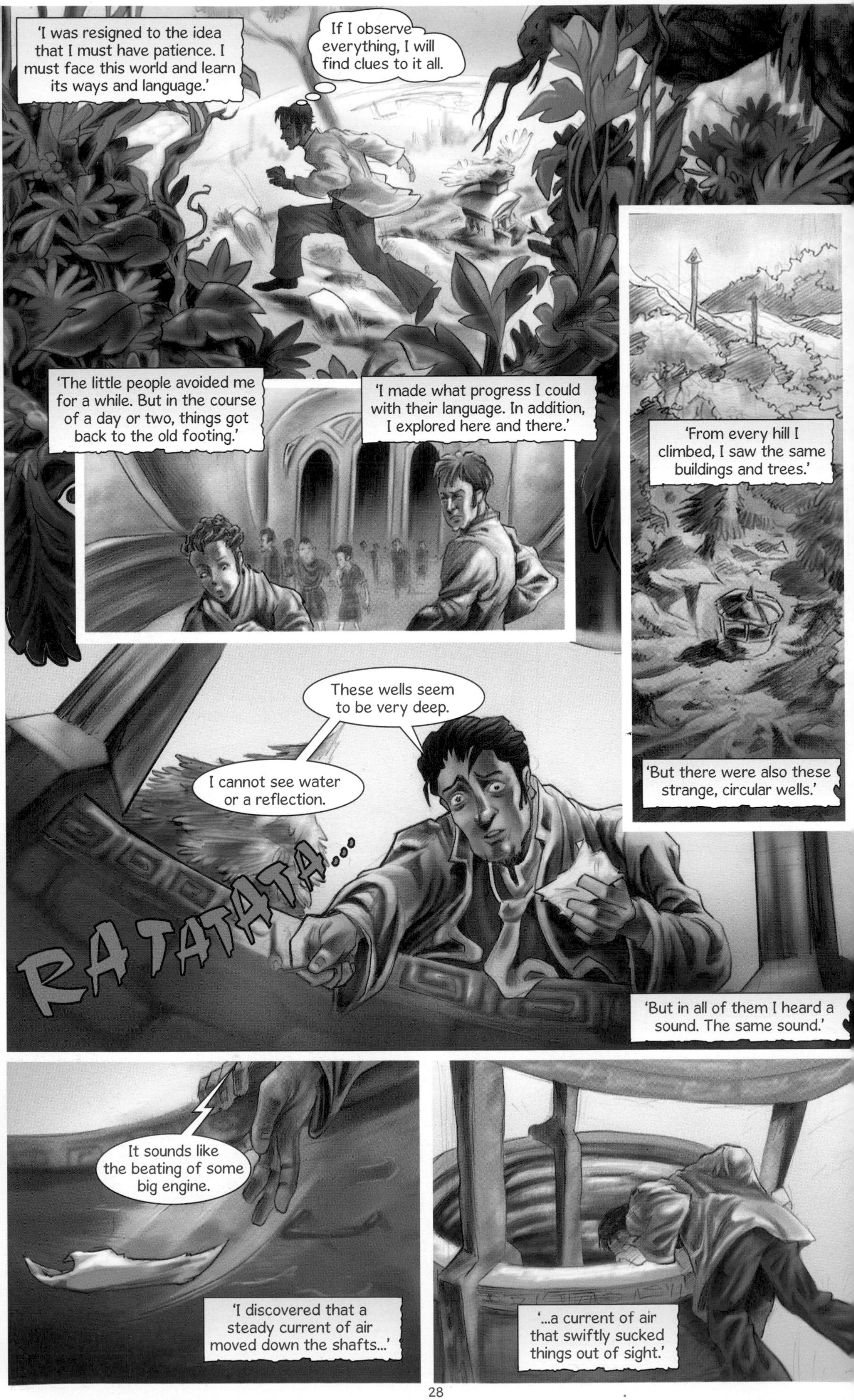
'I was resigned to the idea that I must have patience. I must face this world and learn its ways and language.'
If I observe everything, I will find clues to it all.
'The little people avoided me for a while. But in the course of a day or two, things got back to the old footing.'
'I made what progress I could with their language. In addition, I explored here and there.'
'From every hill I climbed, I saw the same buildings and trees.'
'But there were also these strange, circular wells.'
These wells seem to be very deep.
I cannot see water or a reflection.
RA TATATA...
'But in all of them I heard a sound. The same sound.'
It sounds like the beating of some big engine.
'I discovered that a steady current of air moved down the shafts...'
'...a current of air that swiftly sucked things out of sight.'

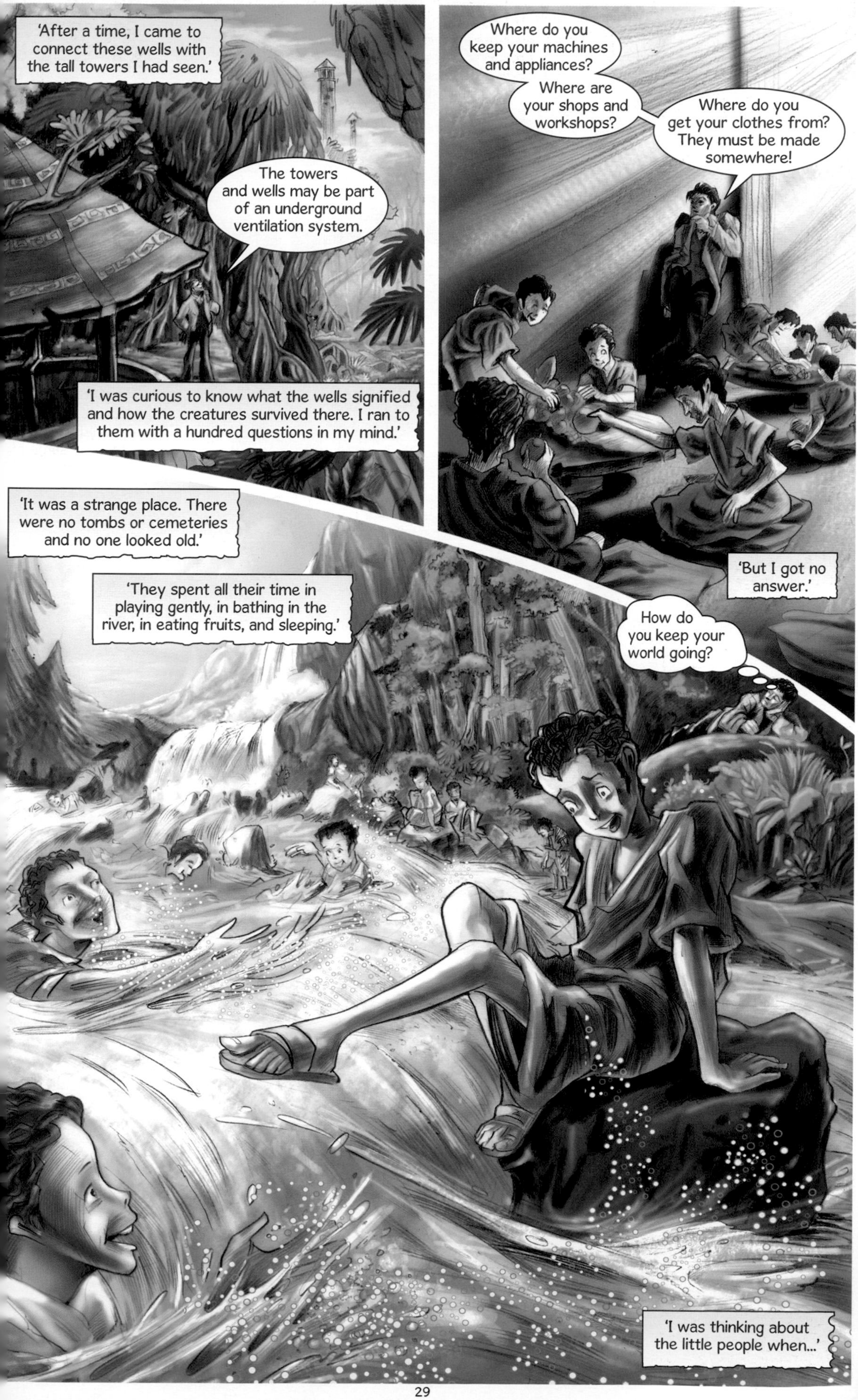
'After a time, I came to connect these wells with the tall towers I had seen.'
The towers and wells may be part of an underground ventilation system.
'I was curious to know what the wells signified and how the creatures survived there. I ran to them with a hundred questions in my mind.'
Where do you keep your machines and appliances?
Where are your shops and workshops?
Where do you get your clothes from? They must be made somewhere!
'It was a strange place. There were no tombs or cemeteries and no one looked old.'
'They spent all their time in playing gently, in bathing in the river, in eating fruits, and sleeping.'
'But I got no answer.'
How do you keep your world going?
'I was thinking about the little people when...'

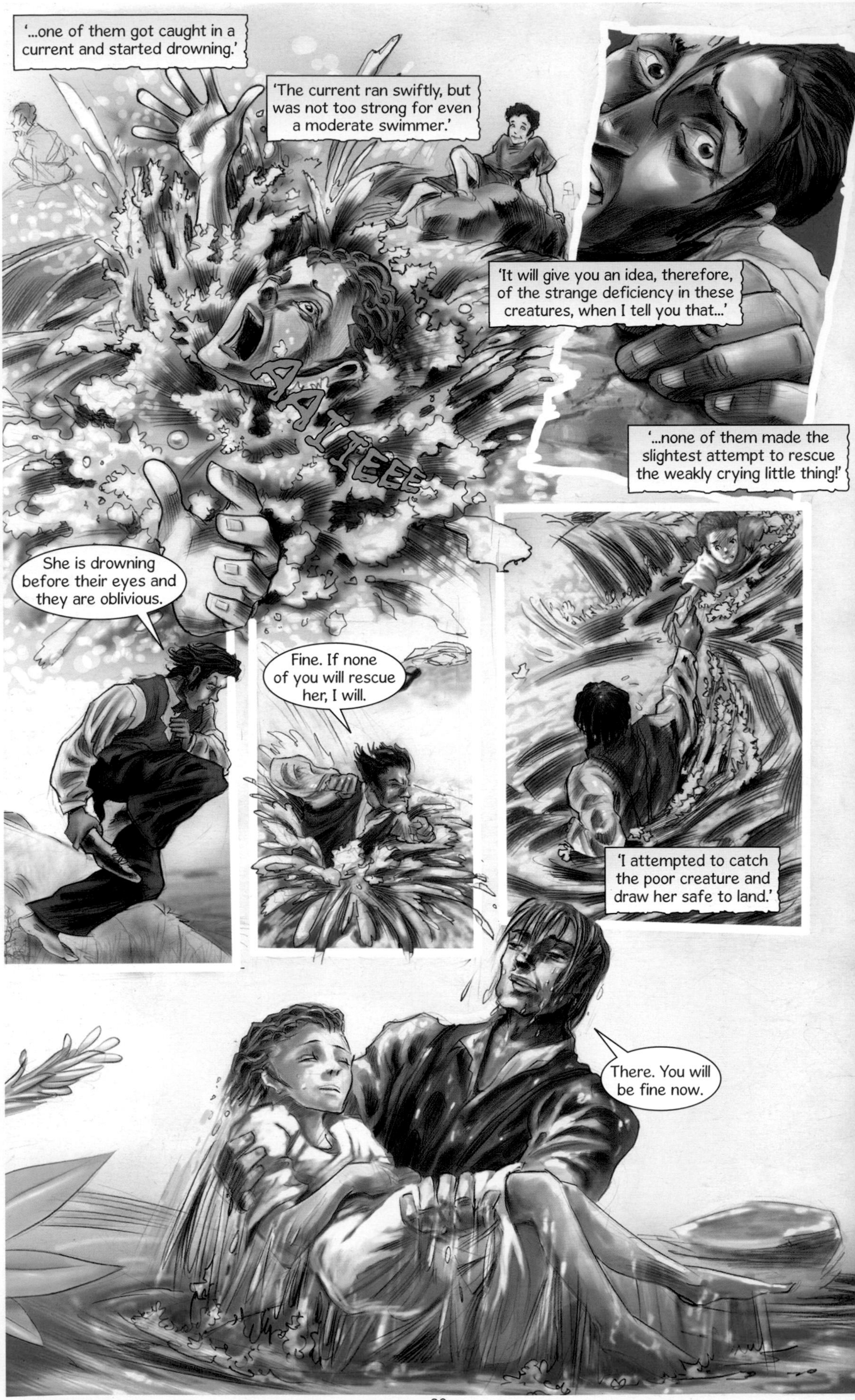
'...one of them got caught in a current and started drowning.'
'The current ran swiftly, but was not too strong for even a moderate swimmer.'
AAIIEEE
'It will give you an idea, therefore, of the strange deficiency in these creatures, when I tell you that...'
'...none of them made the slightest attempt to rescue the weakly crying little thing!'
She is drowning before their eyes and they are oblivious.
Fine. If none of you will rescue her, I will.
'I attempted to catch the poor creature and draw her safe to land.'
There. You will be fine now.

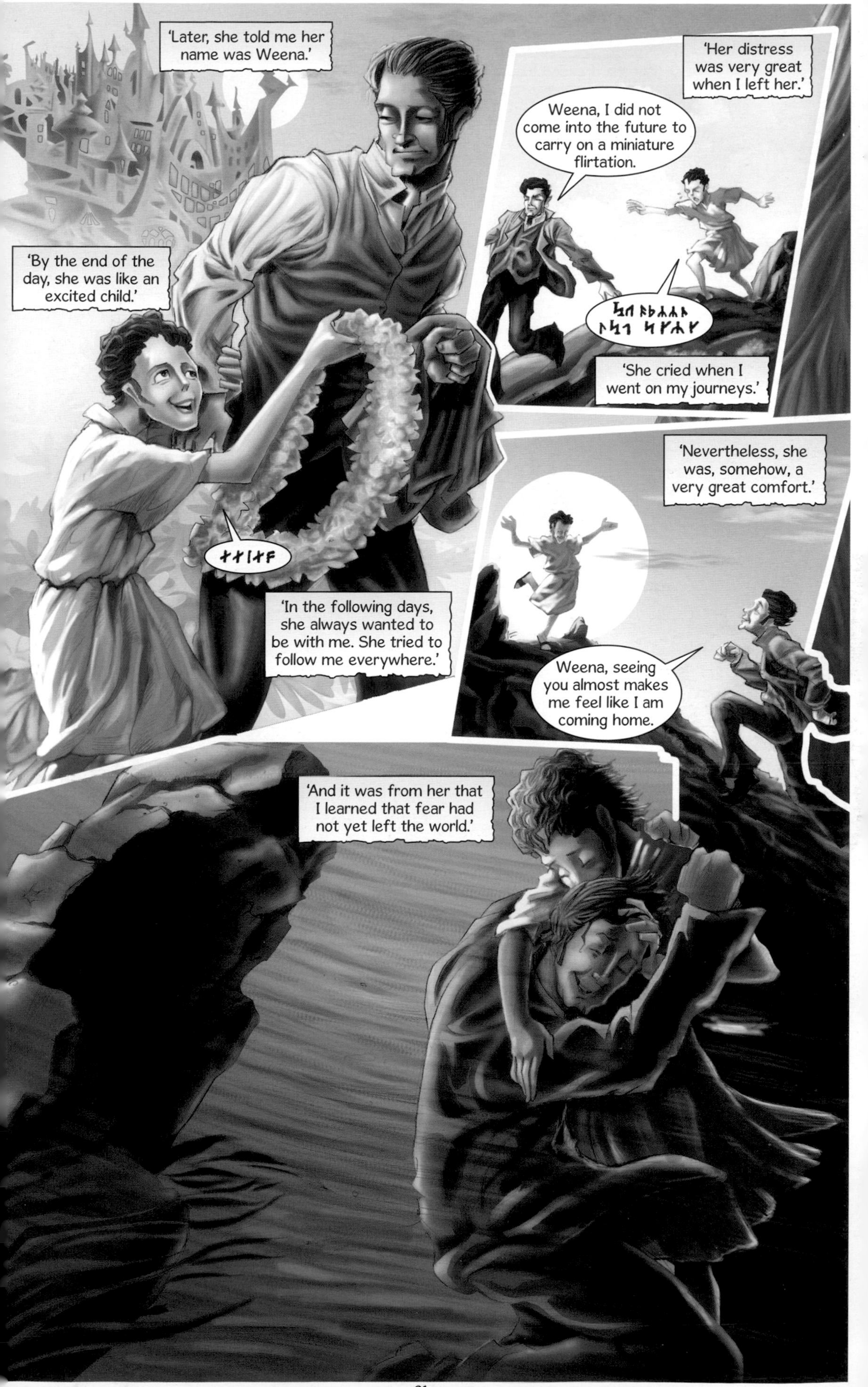
'Later, she told me her name was Weena.'
'By the end of the day, she was like an excited child.'
'In the following days, she always wanted to be with me. She tried to follow me everywhere.'
'Her distress was very great when I left her.'
Weena, I did not come into the future to carry on a miniature flirtation.
'She cried when I went on my journeys.'
'Nevertheless, she was, somehow, a very great comfort.'
Weena, seeing you almost makes me feel like I am coming home.
'And it was from her that I learned that fear had not yet left the world.'

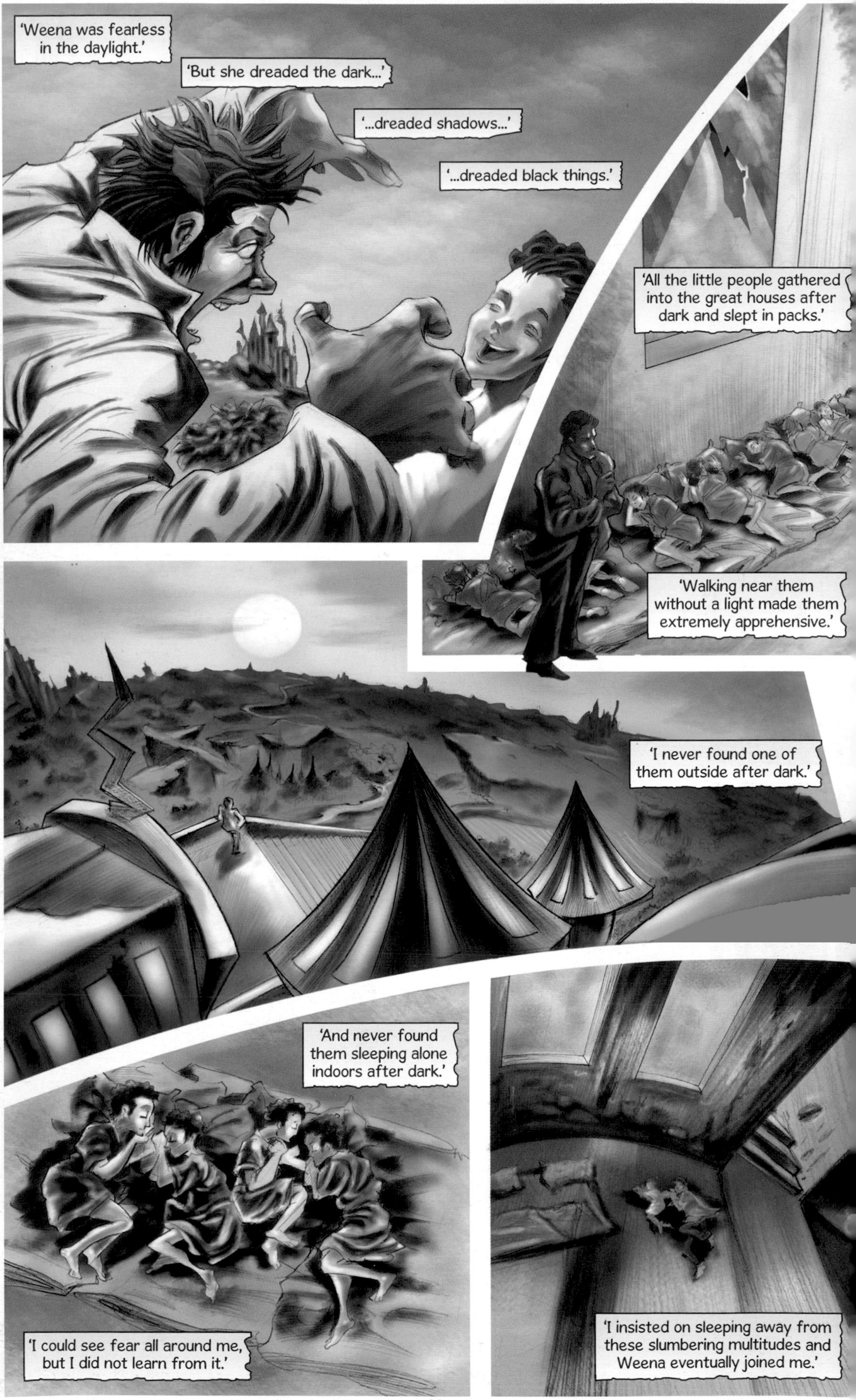

'Weena was fearless in the daylight.'
'But she dreaded the dark...'
'...dreaded shadows...'
'...dreaded black things.'
'All the little people gathered into the great houses after dark and slept in packs.'
'Walking near them without a light made them extremely apprehensive.'
'I never found one of them outside after dark.'
'And never found them sleeping alone indoors after dark.'
'I could see fear all around me, but I did not learn from it.'
'I insisted on sleeping away from these slumbering multitudes and Weena eventually joined me.'

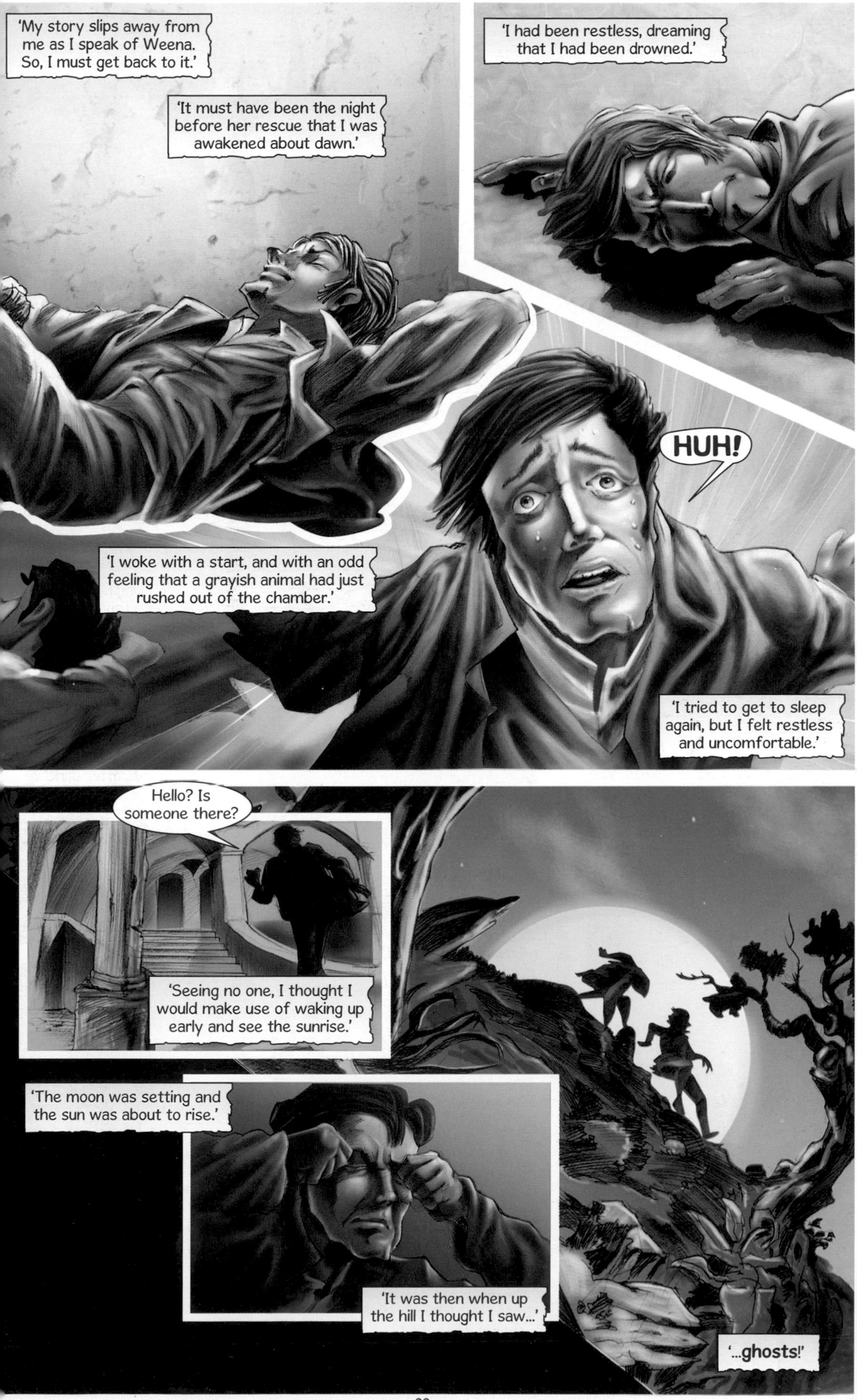
'My story slips away from me as I speak of Weena. So, I must get back to it.'
'It must have been the night before her rescue that I was awakened about dawn.'
'I had been restless, dreaming that I had been drowned.'
HUH!
'I woke with a start, and with an odd feeling that a grayish animal had just rushed out of the chamber.'
'I tried to get to sleep again, but I felt restless and uncomfortable.'
Hello? Is someone there?
'Seeing no one, I thought I would make use of waking up early and see the sunrise.'
'The moon was setting and the sun was about to rise.'
'It was then when up the hill I thought I saw...'
'...ghosts!'

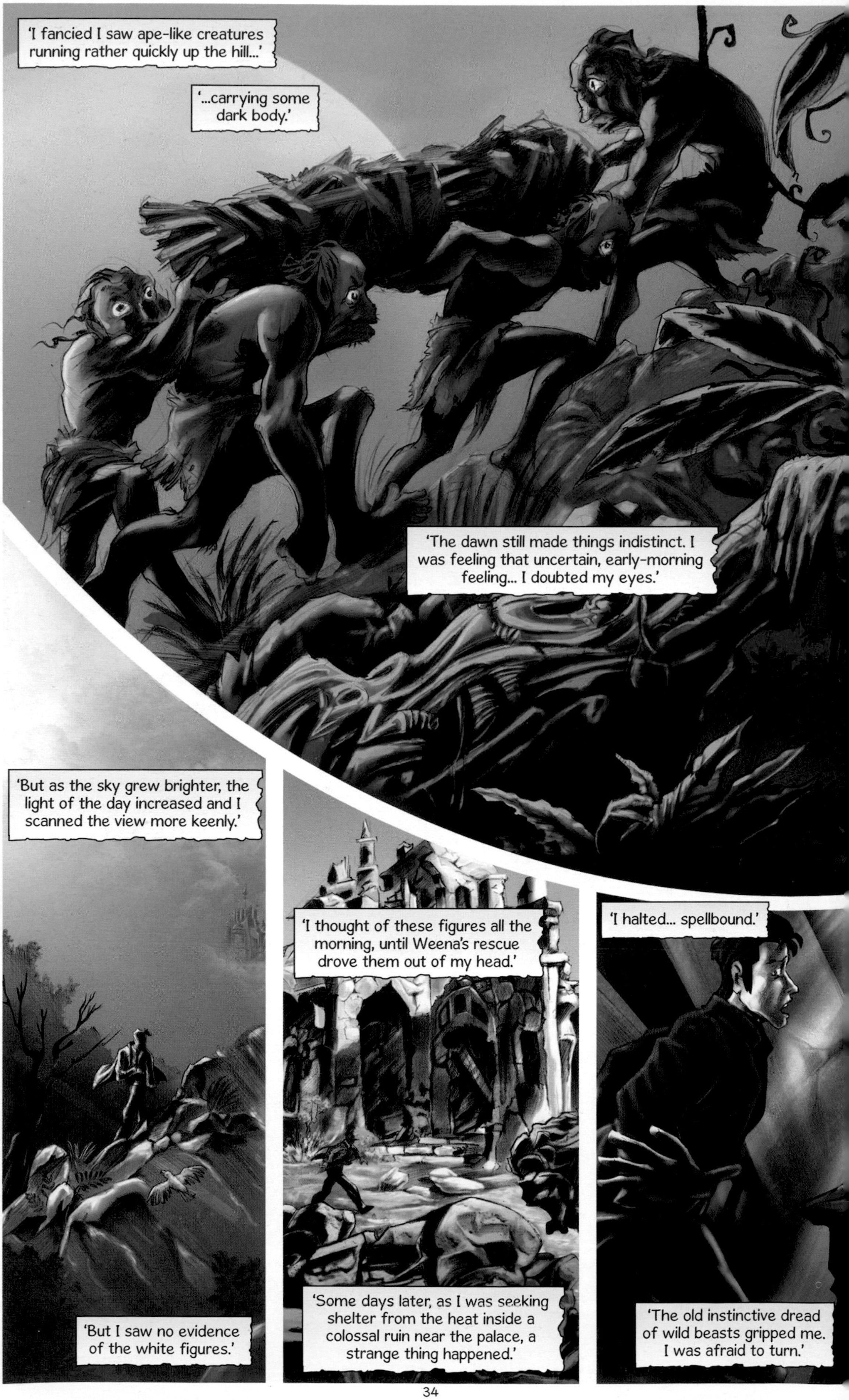
'I fancied I saw ape-like creatures running rather quickly up the hill...'
'...carrying some dark body.'
'The dawn still made things indistinct. I was feeling that uncertain, early-morning feeling... I doubted my eyes.'
'But as the sky grew brighter, the light of the day increased and I scanned the view more keenly.'
'But I saw no evidence of the white figures.'
'I thought of these figures all the morning, until Weena's rescue drove them out of my head.'
'Some days later, as I was seeking shelter from the heat inside a colossal ruin near the palace, a strange thing happened.'
'I halted... spellbound.'
'The old instinctive dread of wild beasts gripped me. I was afraid to turn.'

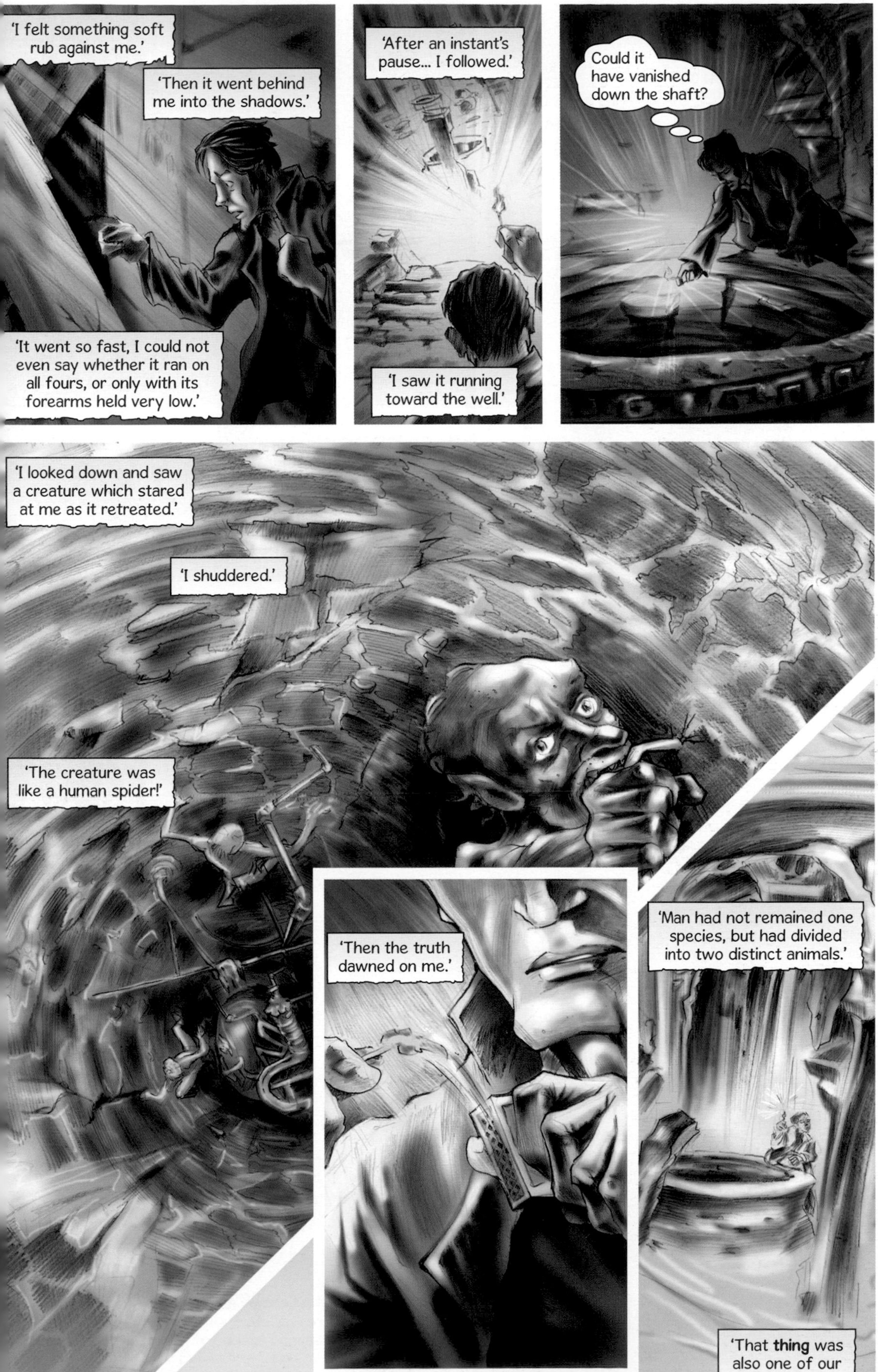
'I felt something soft rub against me.'
'Then it went behind me into the shadows.'
'It went so fast, I could not even say whether it ran on all fours, or only with its forearms held very low.'
'After an instant's pause... I followed.'
'I saw it running toward the well.'
Could it have vanished down the shaft?
'I looked down and saw a creature which stared at me as it retreated.'
'I shuddered.'
'The creature was like a human spider!'
'Then the truth dawned on me.'
'Man had not remained one species, but had divided into two distinct animals.'
'That **thing** was also one of our descendents.'

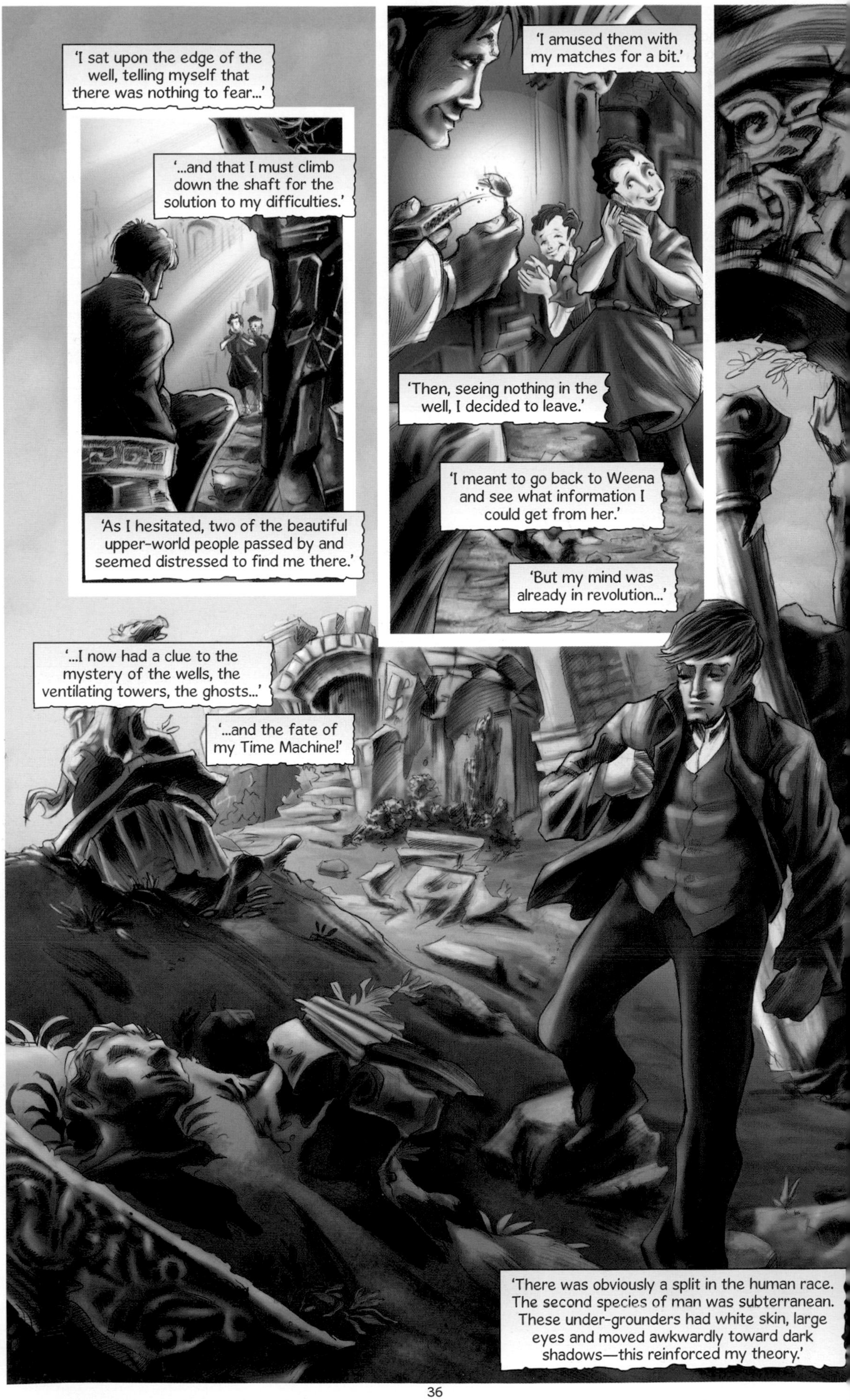

'I sat upon the edge of the well, telling myself that there was nothing to fear...'
'...and that I must climb down the shaft for the solution to my difficulties.'
'As I hesitated, two of the beautiful upper-world people passed by and seemed distressed to find me there.'
'I amused them with my matches for a bit.'
'Then, seeing nothing in the well, I decided to leave.'
'I meant to go back to Weena and see what information I could get from her.'
'But my mind was already in revolution...'
'...I now had a clue to the mystery of the wells, the ventilating towers, the ghosts...'
'...and the fate of my Time Machine!'
'There was obviously a split in the human race. The second species of man was subterranean. These under-grounders had white skin, large eyes and moved awkwardly toward dark shadows—this reinforced my theory.'

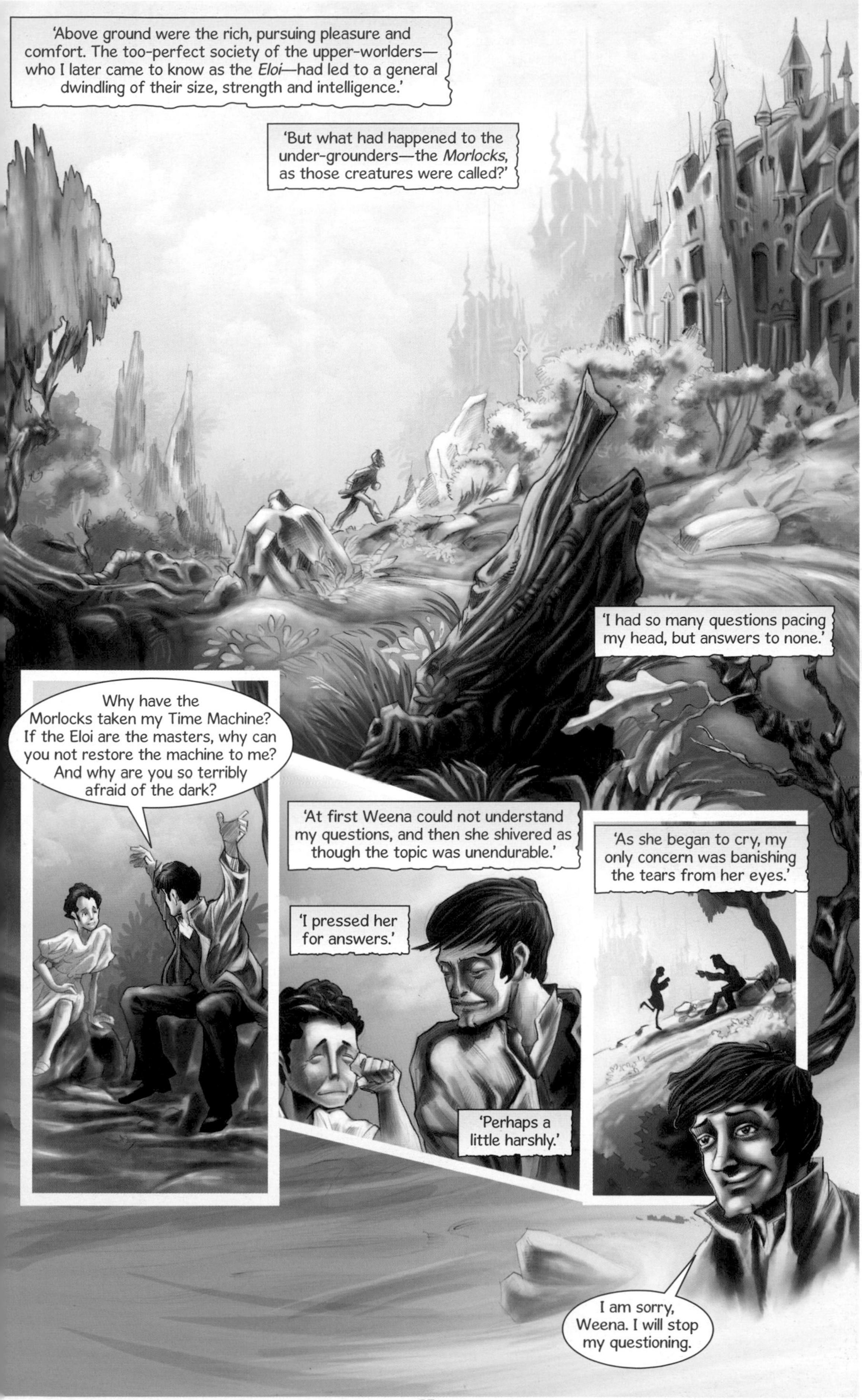

'Above ground were the rich, pursuing pleasure and comfort. The too-perfect society of the upper-worlders—who I later came to know as the *Eloi*—had led to a general dwindling of their size, strength and intelligence.'
'But what had happened to the under-grounders—the *Morlocks*, as those creatures were called?'
'I had so many questions pacing my head, but answers to none.'
Why have the Morlocks taken my Time Machine? If the Eloi are the masters, why can you not restore the machine to me? And why are you so terribly afraid of the dark?
'At first Weena could not understand my questions, and then she shivered as though the topic was unendurable.'
'I pressed her for answers.'
'Perhaps a little harshly.'
'As she began to cry, my only concern was banishing the tears from her eyes.'
I am sorry, Weena. I will stop my questioning.

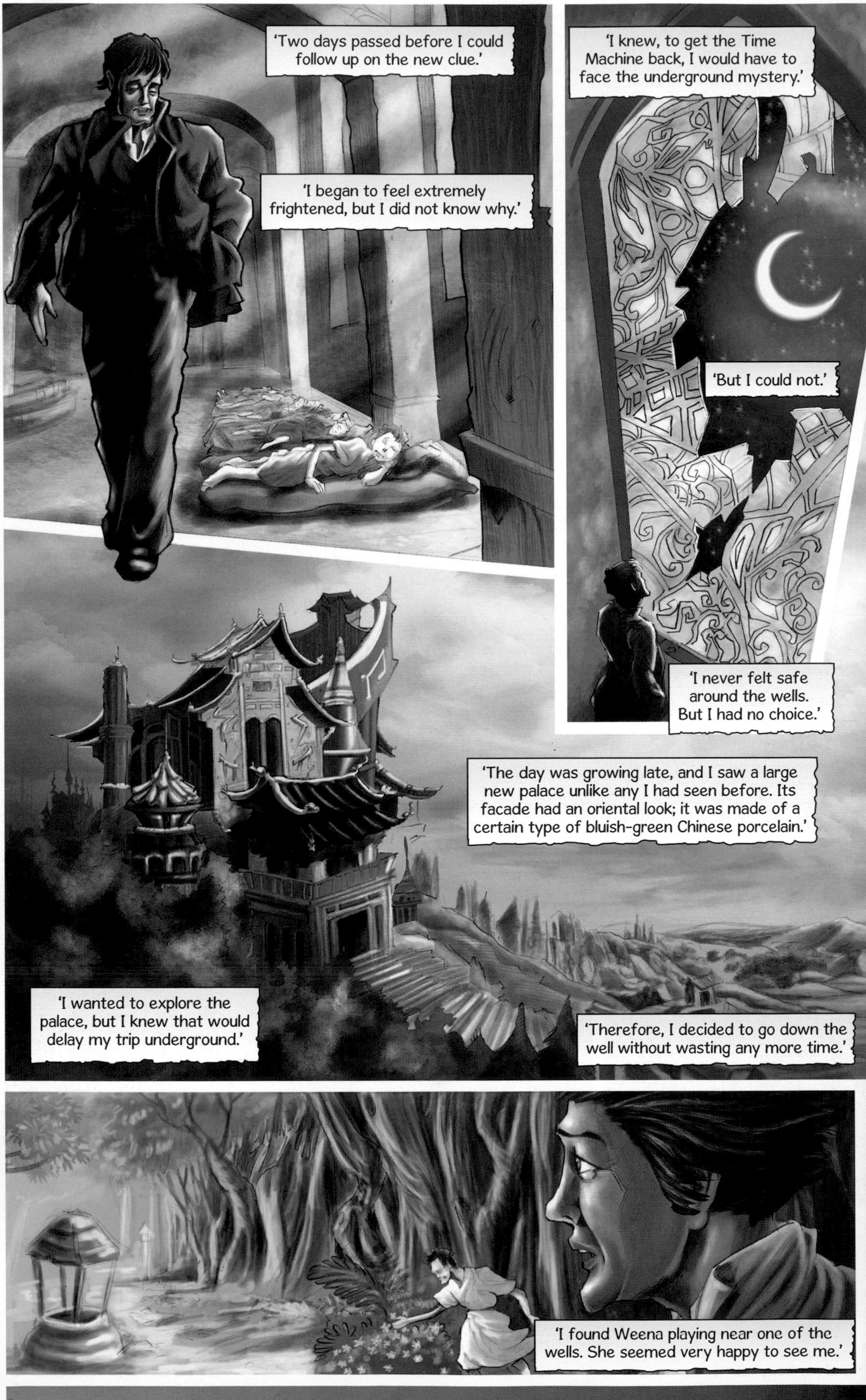
'Two days passed before I could follow up on the new clue.'
'I began to feel extremely frightened, but I did not know why.'
'I knew, to get the Time Machine back, I would have to face the underground mystery.'
'But I could not.'
'I never felt safe around the wells. But I had no choice.'
'The day was growing late, and I saw a large new palace unlike any I had seen before. Its facade had an oriental look; it was made of a certain type of bluish-green Chinese porcelain.'
'I wanted to explore the palace, but I knew that would delay my trip underground.'
'Therefore, I decided to go down the well without wasting any more time.'
'I found Weena playing near one of the wells. She seemed very happy to see me.'

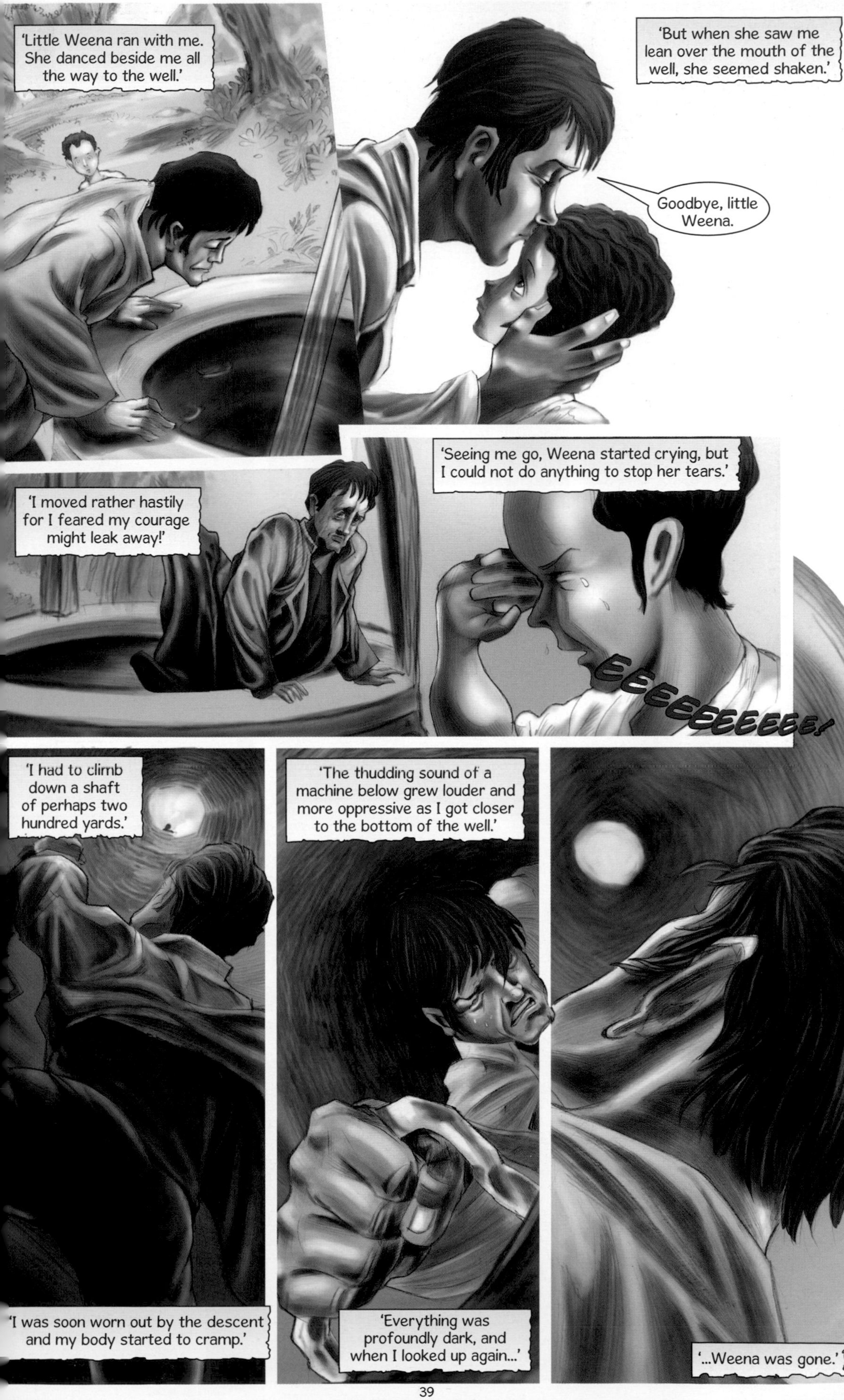
'Little Weena ran with me. She danced beside me all the way to the well.'
'But when she saw me lean over the mouth of the well, she seemed shaken.'
Goodbye, little Weena.
'I moved rather hastily for I feared my courage might leak away!'
'Seeing me go, Weena started crying, but I could not do anything to stop her tears.'
EEEEEEEEEEEEE!
'I had to climb down a shaft of perhaps two hundred yards.'
'I was soon worn out by the descent and my body started to cramp.'
'The thudding sound of a machine below grew louder and more oppressive as I got closer to the bottom of the well.'
'Everything was profoundly dark, and when I looked up again...'
'...Weena was gone.'

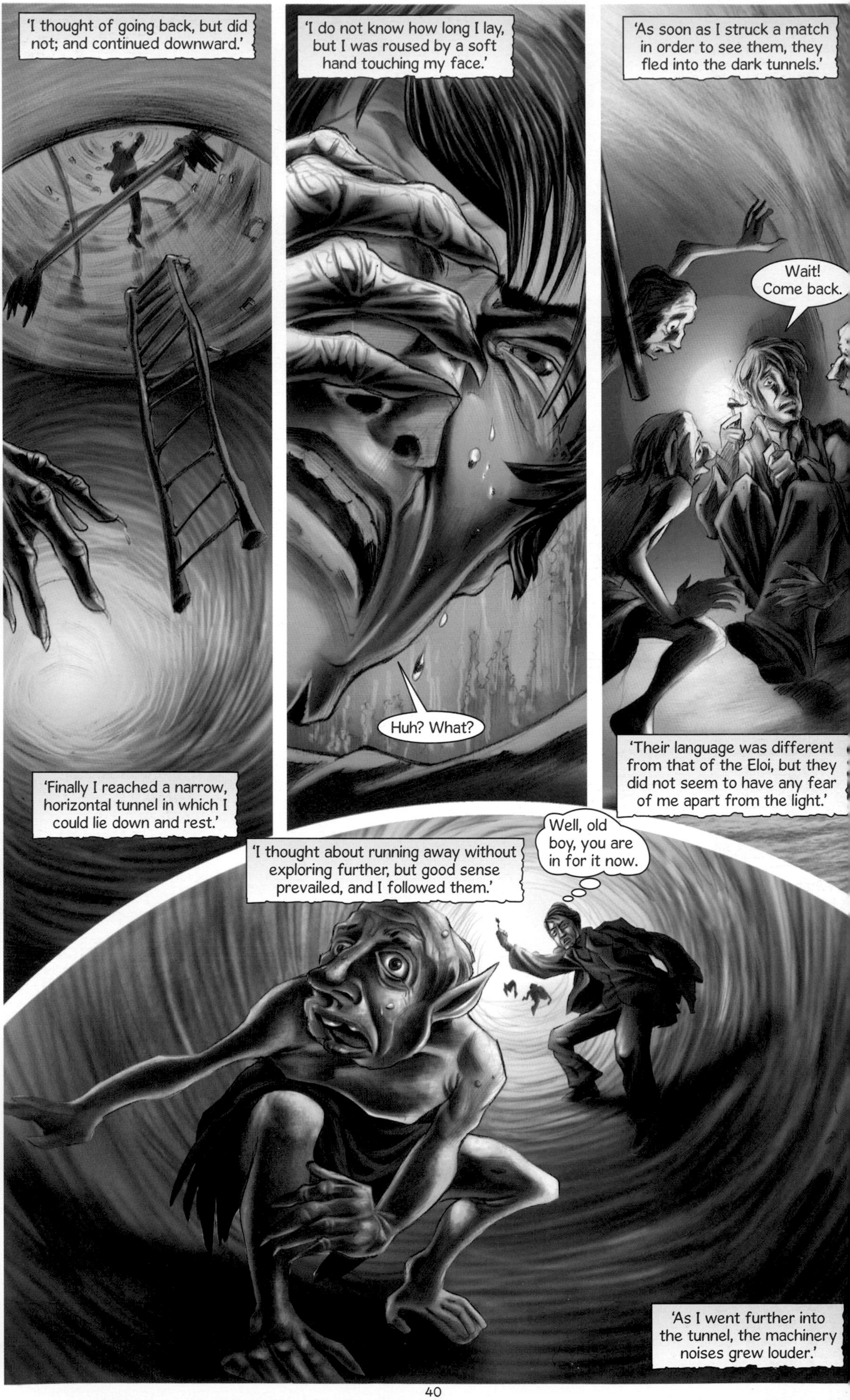
'I thought of going back, but did not; and continued downward.'
'Finally I reached a narrow, horizontal tunnel in which I could lie down and rest.'
'I do not know how long I lay, but I was roused by a soft hand touching my face.'
Huh? What?
'As soon as I struck a match in order to see them, they fled into the dark tunnels.'
Wait! Come back.
'Their language was different from that of the Eloi, but they did not seem to have any fear of me apart from the light.'
'I thought about running away without exploring further, but good sense prevailed, and I followed them.'
Well, old boy, you are in for it now.
'As I went further into the tunnel, the machinery noises grew louder.'

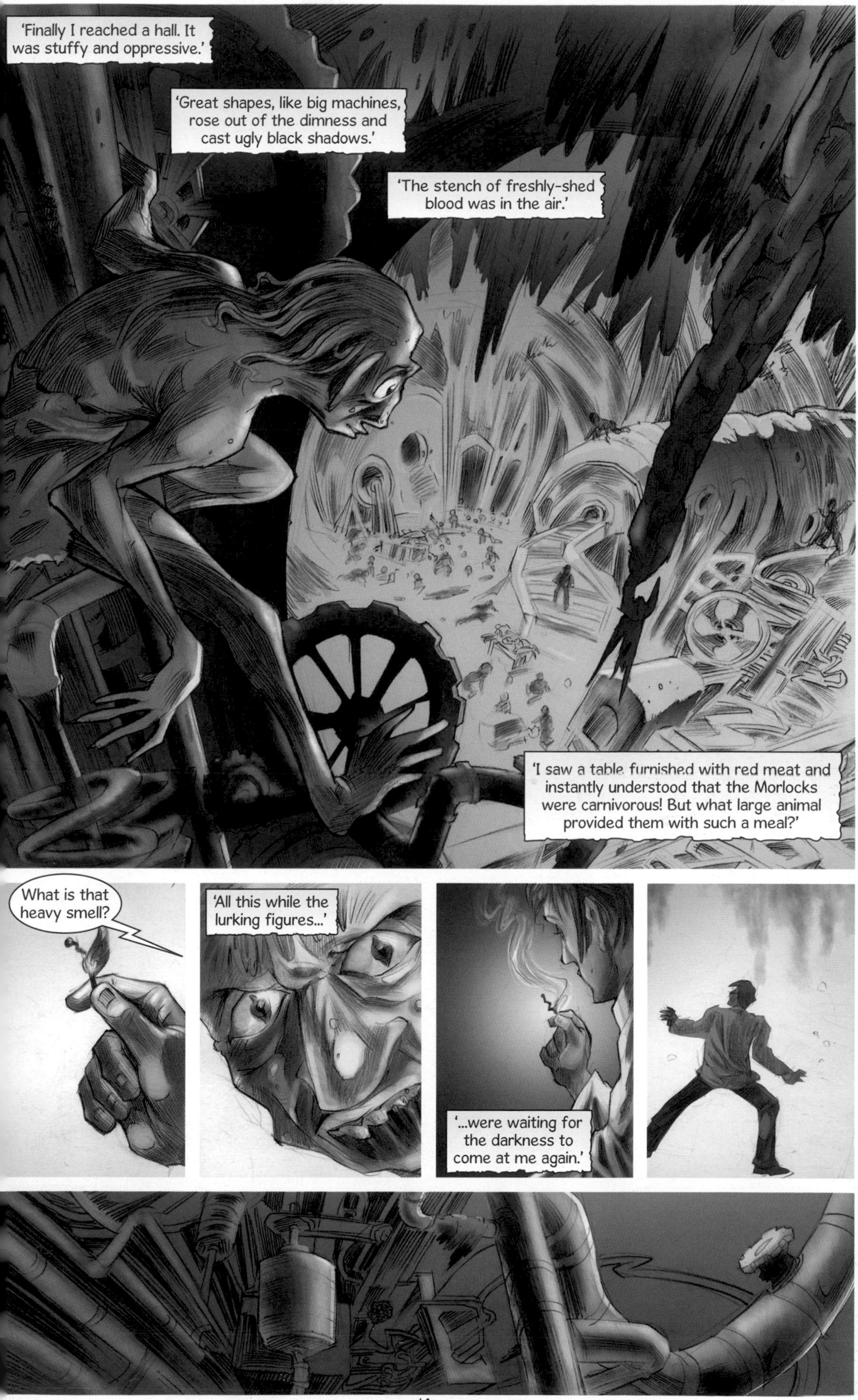
'Finally I reached a hall. It was stuffy and oppressive.'
'Great shapes, like big machines, rose out of the dimness and cast ugly black shadows.'
'The stench of freshly-shed blood was in the air.'
'I saw a table furnished with red meat and instantly understood that the Morlocks were carnivorous! But what large animal provided them with such a meal?'
What is that heavy smell?
'All this while the lurking figures...'
'...were waiting for the darkness to come at me again.'

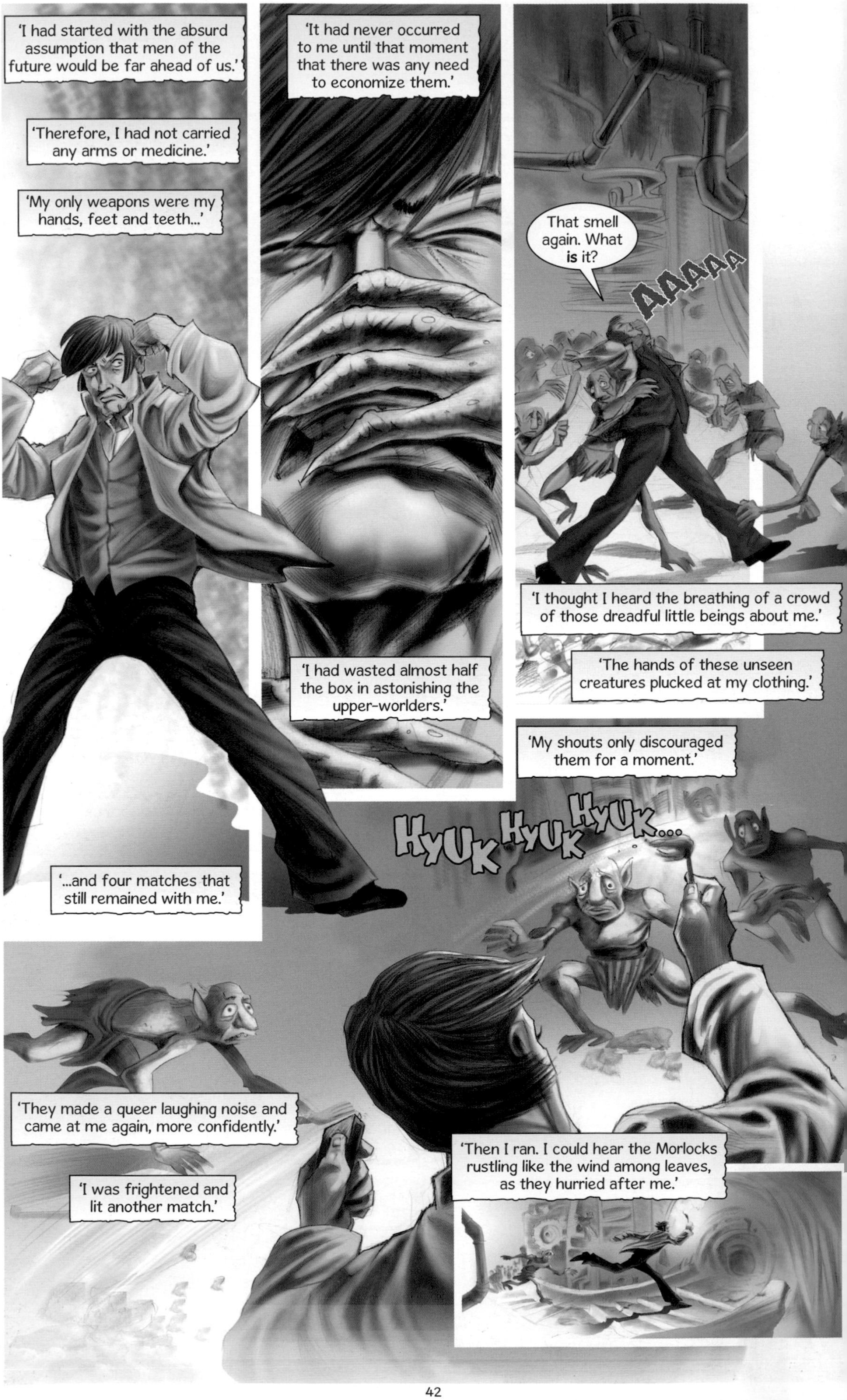
'I had started with the absurd assumption that men of the future would be far ahead of us.'
'Therefore, I had not carried any arms or medicine.'
'My only weapons were my hands, feet and teeth...'
'...and four matches that still remained with me.'
'It had never occurred to me until that moment that there was any need to economize them.'
'I had wasted almost half the box in astonishing the upper-worlders.'
That smell again. What **is** it?
AAAAA
'I thought I heard the breathing of a crowd of those dreadful little beings about me.'
'The hands of these unseen creatures plucked at my clothing.'
'My shouts only discouraged them for a moment.'
HYUK HYUK HYUK...
'They made a queer laughing noise and came at me again, more confidently.'
'I was frightened and lit another match.'
'Then I ran. I could hear the Morlocks rustling like the wind among leaves, as they hurried after me.'

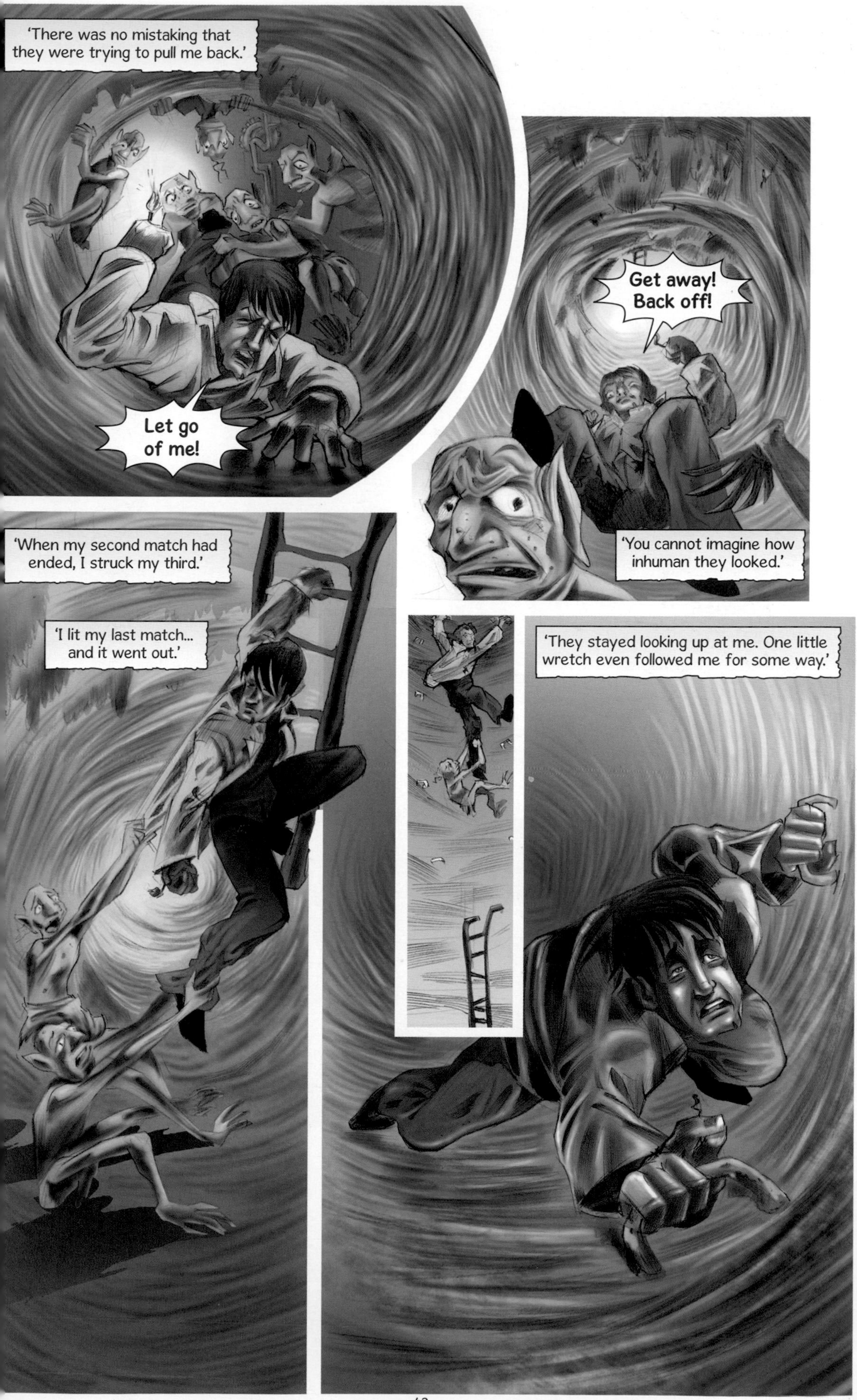
'There was no mistaking that they were trying to pull me back.'
Let go of me!
Get away! Back off!
'You cannot imagine how inhuman they looked.'
'When my second match had ended, I struck my third.'
'I lit my last match... and it went out.'
'They stayed looking up at me. One little wretch even followed me for some way.'

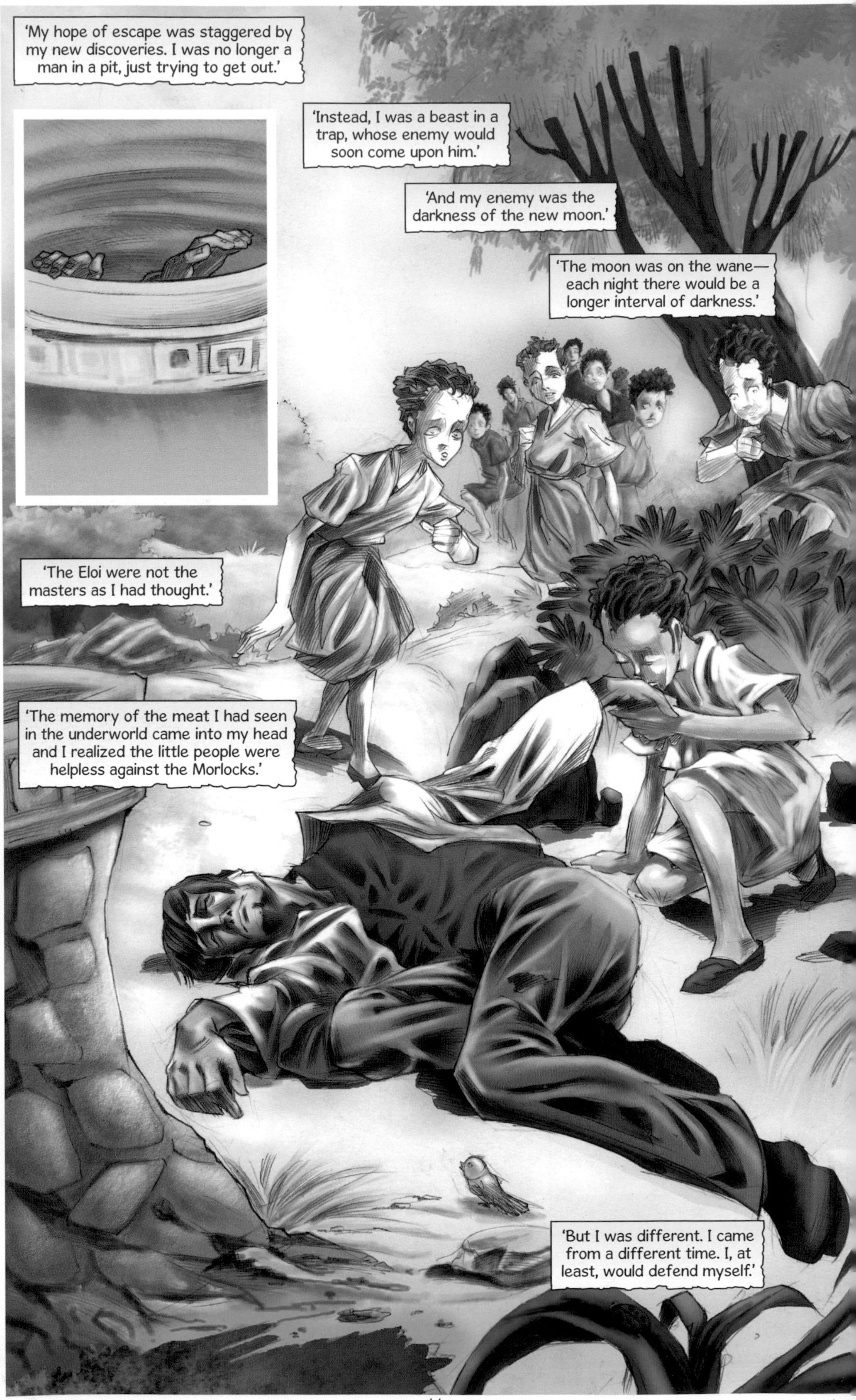
'My hope of escape was staggered by my new discoveries. I was no longer a man in a pit, just trying to get out.'
'Instead, I was a beast in a trap, whose enemy would soon come upon him.'
'And my enemy was the darkness of the new moon.'
'The moon was on the wane—each night there would be a longer interval of darkness.'
'The Eloi were not the masters as I had thought.'
'The memory of the meat I had seen in the underworld came into my head and I realized the little people were helpless against the Morlocks.'
'But I was different. I came from a different time. I, at least, would defend myself.'

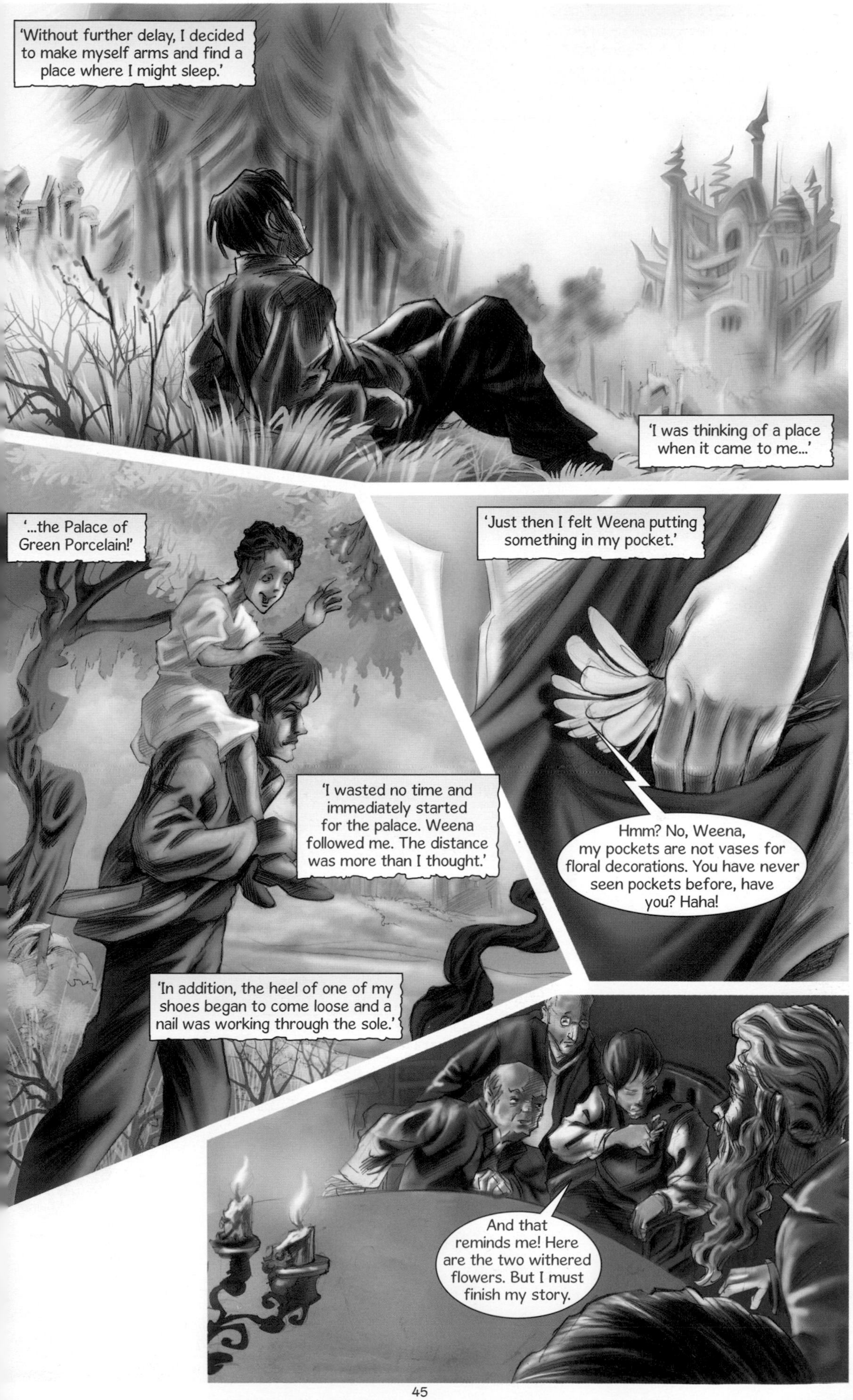
'Without further delay, I decided to make myself arms and find a place where I might sleep.'
'I was thinking of a place when it came to me...'
'...the Palace of Green Porcelain!'
'I wasted no time and immediately started for the palace. Weena followed me. The distance was more than I thought.'
'In addition, the heel of one of my shoes began to come loose and a nail was working through the sole.'
'Just then I felt Weena putting something in my pocket.'
Hmm? No, Weena, my pockets are not vases for floral decorations. You have never seen pockets before, have you? Haha!
And that reminds me! Here are the two withered flowers. But I must finish my story.

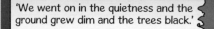
'We went on in the quietness and the ground grew dim and the trees black.'

I can no longer see the Palace of Green Porcelain, Weena.

Which direction is it in?

'Weena's fears and her fatigue grew upon her.'

'I was tired of walking endlessly, so I decided to spend the night on a cliff.'

'Man, as I knew him, had been swept out of existence.'

'And with a sudden shiver...'

'...came the clear knowledge of what the meat I had seen could have been...'

'There were just these fragile creatures and the white things.'

'Then I thought of the great fear between the two species.'

'...the Eloi... it was too horrible!'

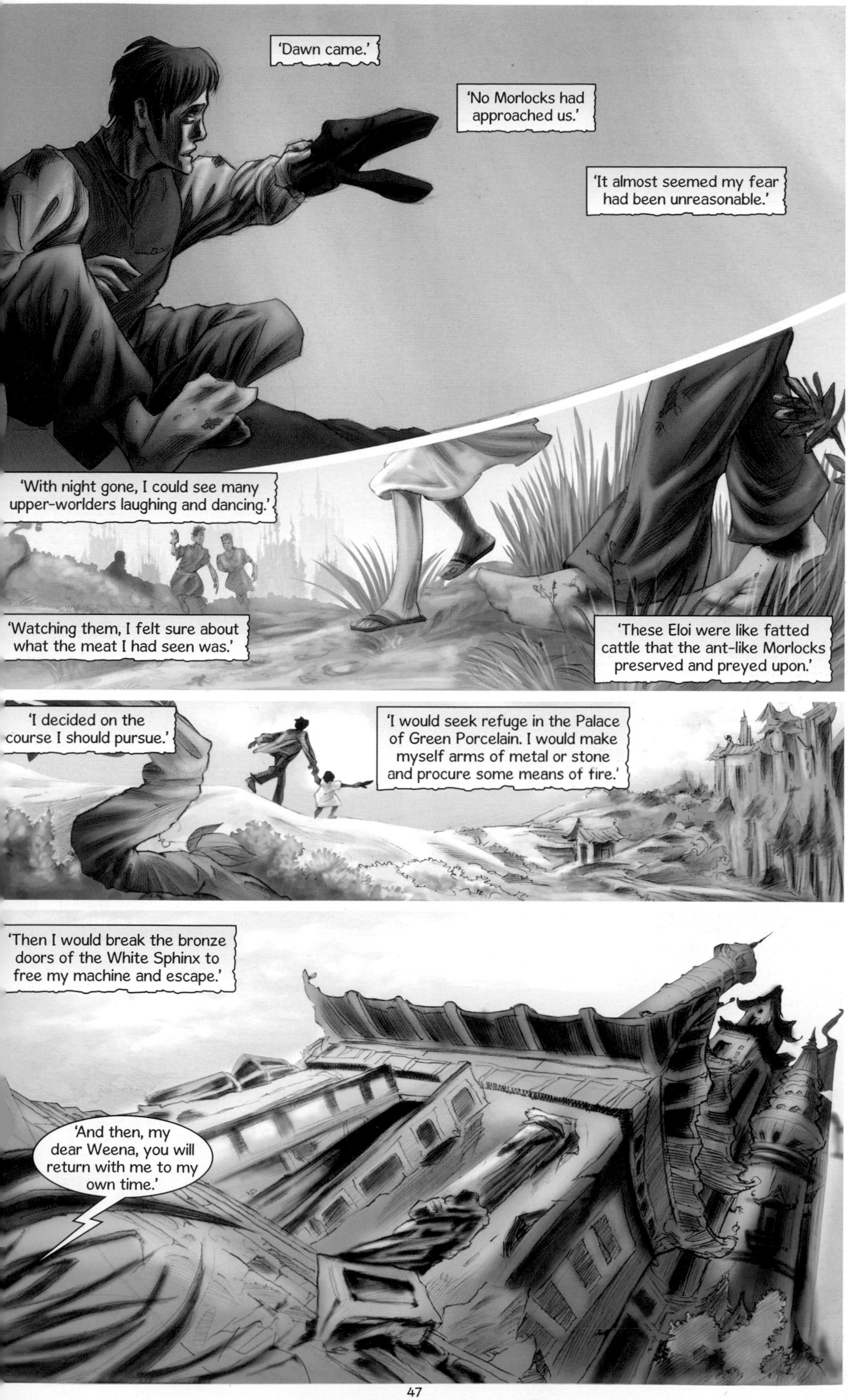
'Dawn came.'
'No Morlocks had approached us.'
'It almost seemed my fear had been unreasonable.'
'With night gone, I could see many upper-worlders laughing and dancing.'
'Watching them, I felt sure about what the meat I had seen was.'
'These Eloi were like fatted cattle that the ant-like Morlocks preserved and preyed upon.'
'I decided on the course I should pursue.'
'I would seek refuge in the Palace of Green Porcelain. I would make myself arms of metal or stone and procure some means of fire.'
'Then I would break the bronze doors of the White Sphinx to free my machine and escape.'
'And then, my dear Weena, you will return with me to my own time.'

'After deciding my course of action, I almost ran to the palace.'

'It had once been a museum. There were galleries filled with minerals, desiccated mummies in jars and huge machines.'

'I was so surprised by this ancient monument that I gave no thought to the possibilities it presented.'

'And was so busy thinking about the machines that I did not notice the light diminishing.'

'Weena's increasing apprehensions drew my attention to the darkness.'

'Just then I heard a peculiar pattering—the same odd noises I had heard down the well. And I observed a number of footprints.'

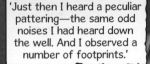

'You may think it inhuman but...'

'...I longed to kill a Morlock! It was impossible to feel any humanity toward them.'

'I pulled a metal bar from an old machine, and decided to use it as my weapon against the Morlocks.'

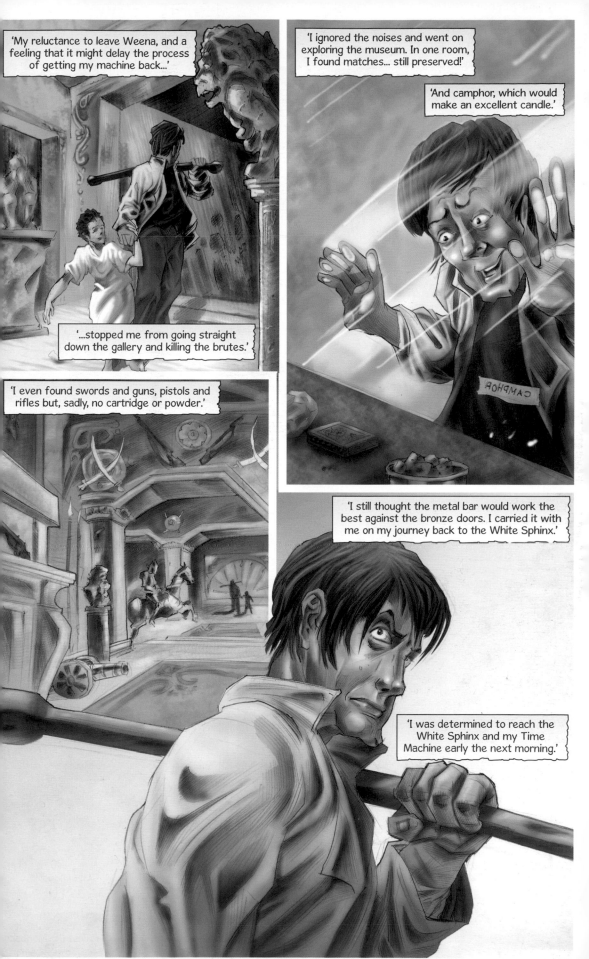

'My reluctance to leave Weena, and a feeling that it might delay the process of getting my machine back...'

'...stopped me from going straight down the gallery and killing the brutes.'

'I even found swords and guns, pistols and rifles but, sadly, no cartridge or powder.'

'I ignored the noises and went on exploring the museum. In one room, I found matches... still preserved!'

'And camphor, which would make an excellent candle.'

'I still thought the metal bar would work the best against the bronze doors. I carried it with me on my journey back to the White Sphinx.'

'I was determined to reach the White Sphinx and my Time Machine early the next morning.'

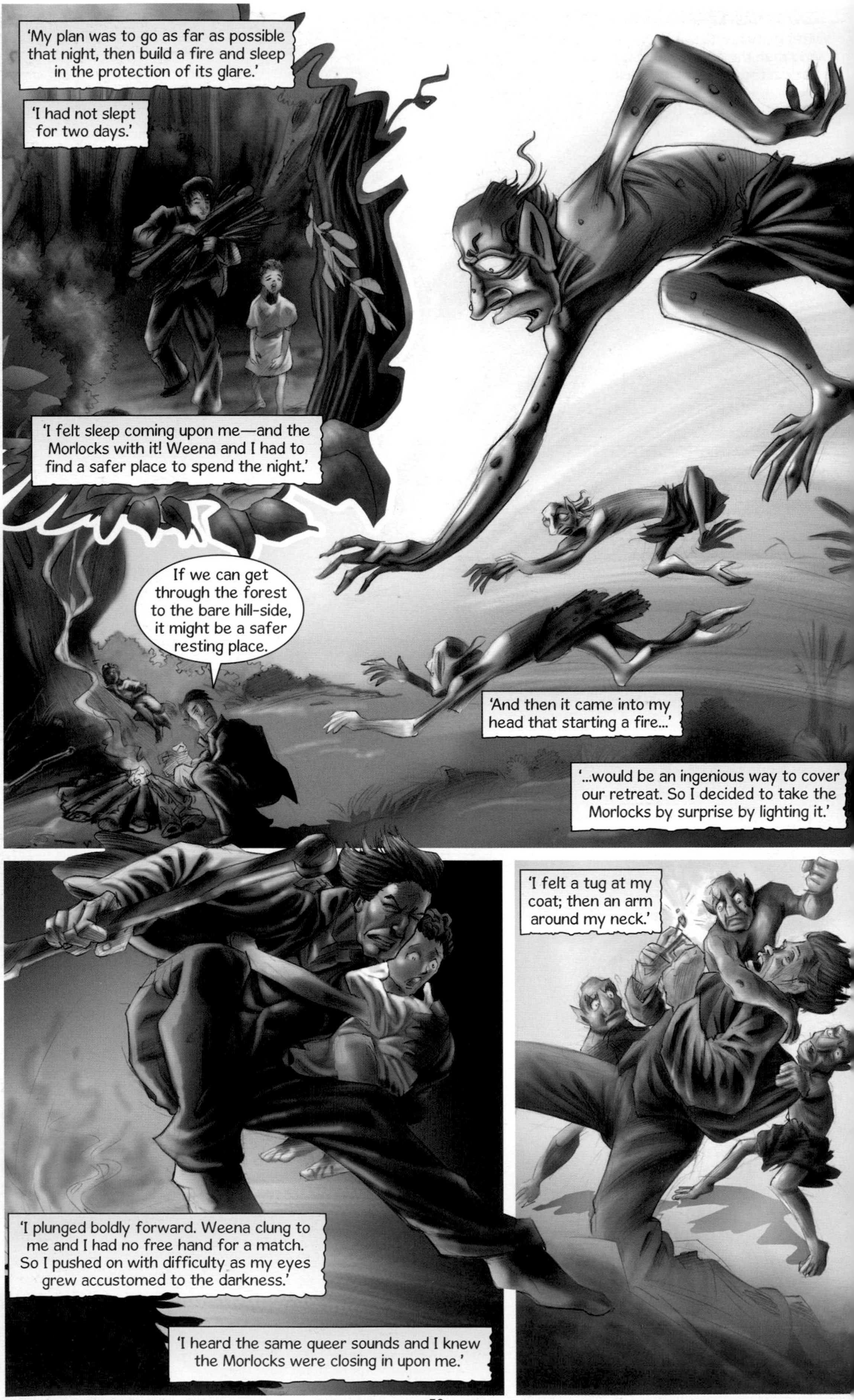

'My plan was to go as far as possible that night, then build a fire and sleep in the protection of its glare.'
'I had not slept for two days.'
'I felt sleep coming upon me—and the Morlocks with it! Weena and I had to find a safer place to spend the night.'
If we can get through the forest to the bare hill-side, it might be a safer resting place.
'And then it came into my head that starting a fire...'
'...would be an ingenious way to cover our retreat. So I decided to take the Morlocks by surprise by lighting it.'
'I plunged boldly forward. Weena clung to me and I had no free hand for a match. So I pushed on with difficulty as my eyes grew accustomed to the darkness.'
'I heard the same queer sounds and I knew the Morlocks were closing in upon me.'
'I felt a tug at my coat; then an arm around my neck.'

'The lit camphor flared up and drove the Morlocks back in the shadows.'

'The wood behind seemed full of the stir and murmur of a thousand creatures!'

'...and when I opened them, I was surrounded by many creepy creatures. In a moment I knew what had happened.'

'I had slept.'

'Soon I had a choking smoky fire that would not need replenishing for an hour or so.'

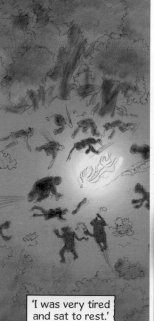

'I was glad that Weena and I were safe. But then came the realization... I had lost my way.'

'I was very tired and sat to rest.'

'I put Weena down upon a piece of turf and began collecting sticks and leaves.'

'I closed my eyes for a second...'

'The fire had gone out and my matches were gone!'

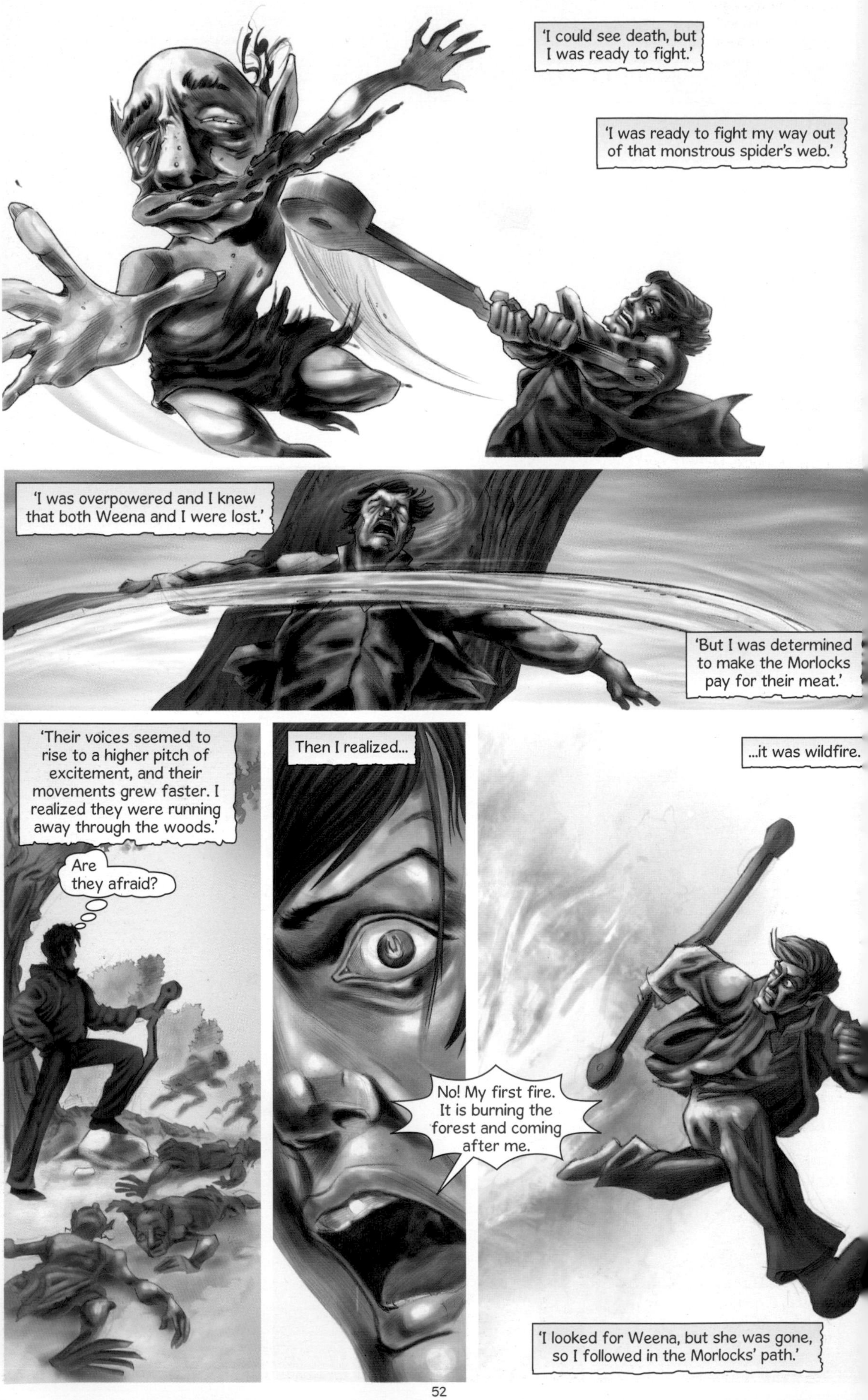
'I could see death, but I was ready to fight.'
'I was ready to fight my way out of that monstrous spider's web.'
'I was overpowered and I knew that both Weena and I were lost.'
'But I was determined to make the Morlocks pay for their meat.'
'Their voices seemed to rise to a higher pitch of excitement, and their movements grew faster. I realized they were running away through the woods.'
Are they afraid?
Then I realized...
No! My first fire. It is burning the forest and coming after me.
...it was wildfire.
'I looked for Weena, but she was gone, so I followed in the Morlocks' path.'

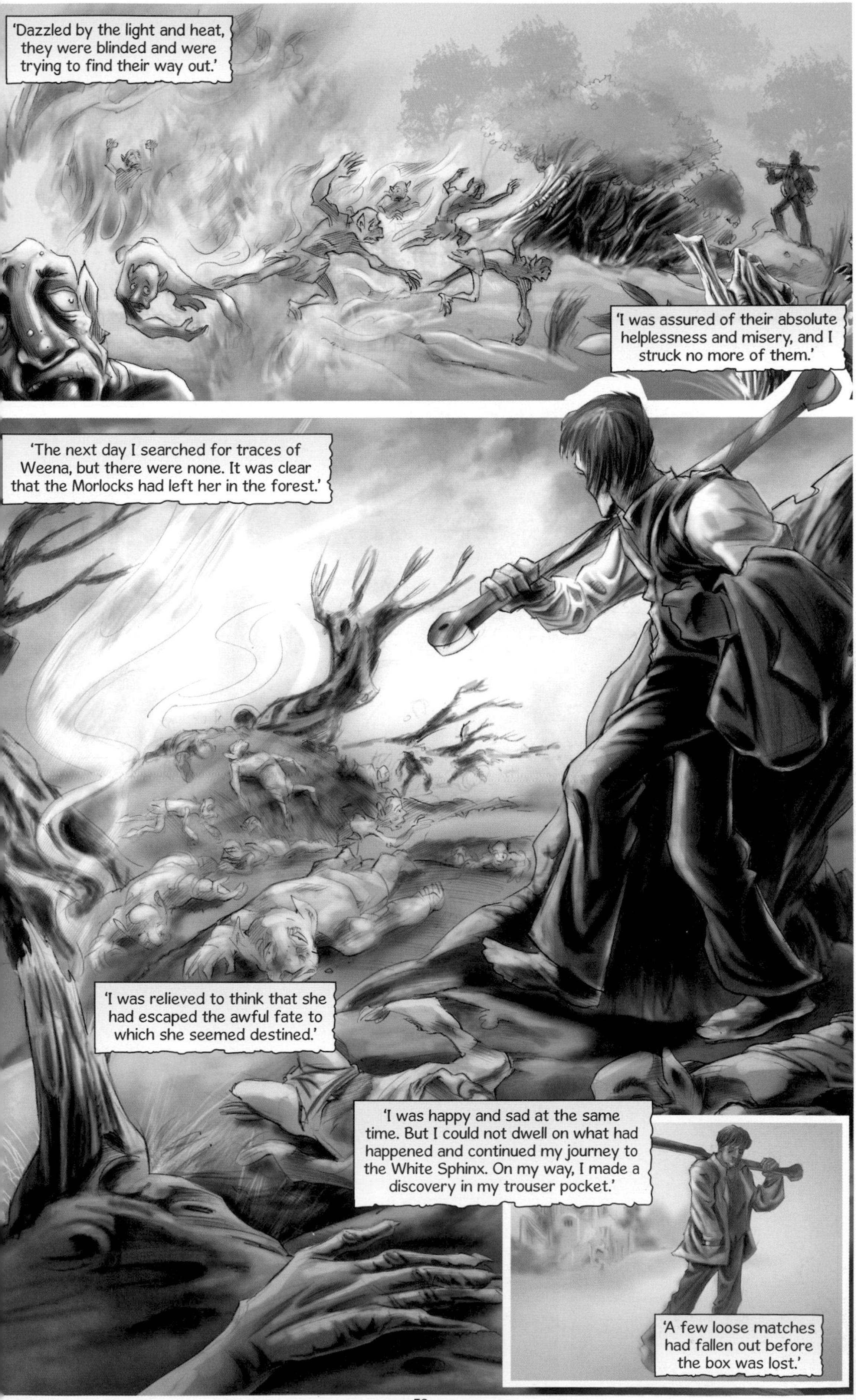
'Dazzled by the light and heat, they were blinded and were trying to find their way out.'
'I was assured of their absolute helplessness and misery, and I struck no more of them.'
'The next day I searched for traces of Weena, but there were none. It was clear that the Morlocks had left her in the forest.'
'I was relieved to think that she had escaped the awful fate to which she seemed destined.'
'I was happy and sad at the same time. But I could not dwell on what had happened and continued my journey to the White Sphinx. On my way, I made a discovery in my trouser pocket.'
'A few loose matches had fallen out before the box was lost.'

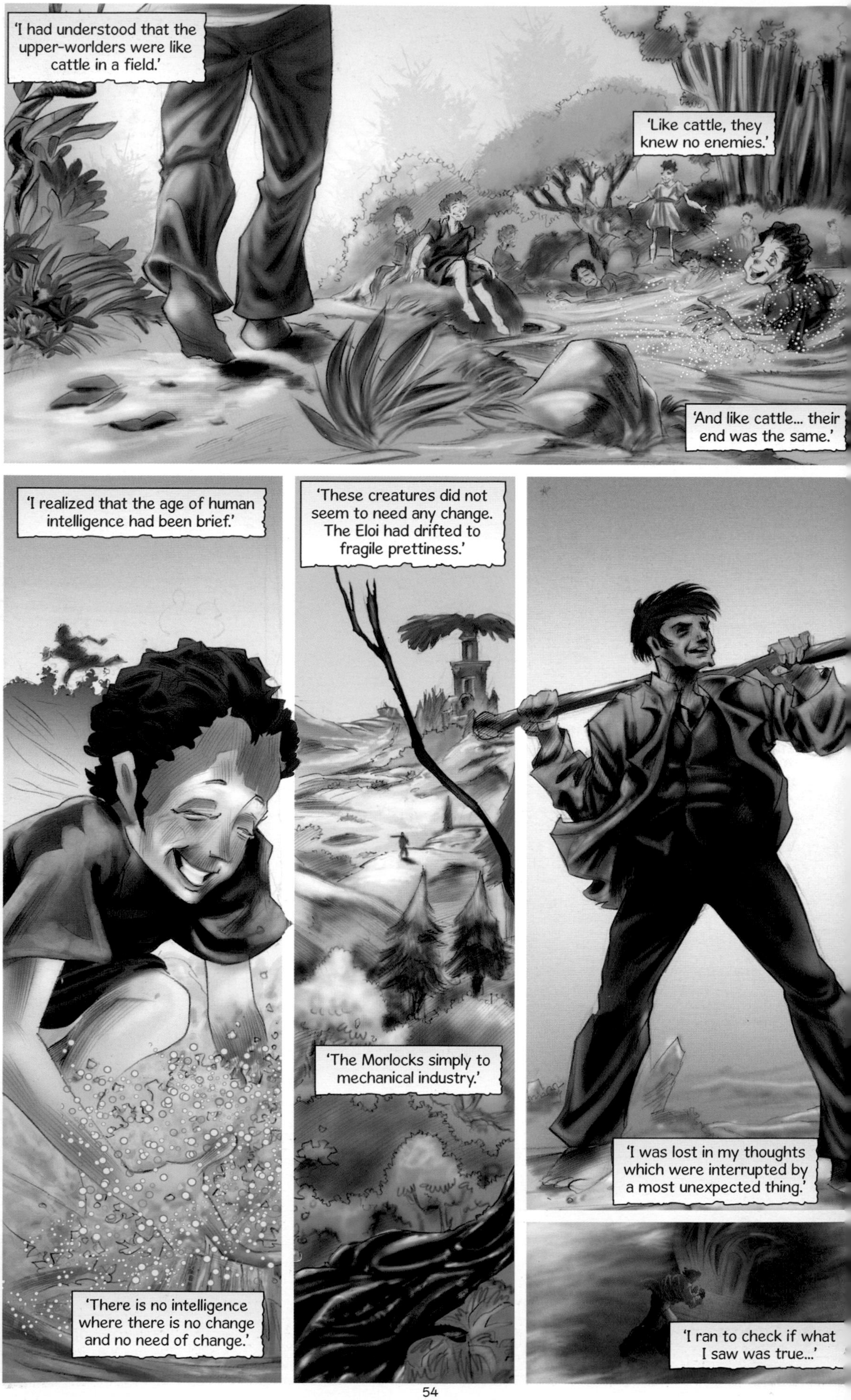
'I had understood that the upper-worlders were like cattle in a field.'
'Like cattle, they knew no enemies.'
'And like cattle... their end was the same.'
'I realized that the age of human intelligence had been brief.'
'There is no intelligence where there is no change and no need of change.'
'These creatures did not seem to need any change. The Eloi had drifted to fragile prettiness.'
'The Morlocks simply to mechanical industry.'
'I was lost in my thoughts which were interrupted by a most unexpected thing.'
'I ran to check if what I saw was true...'

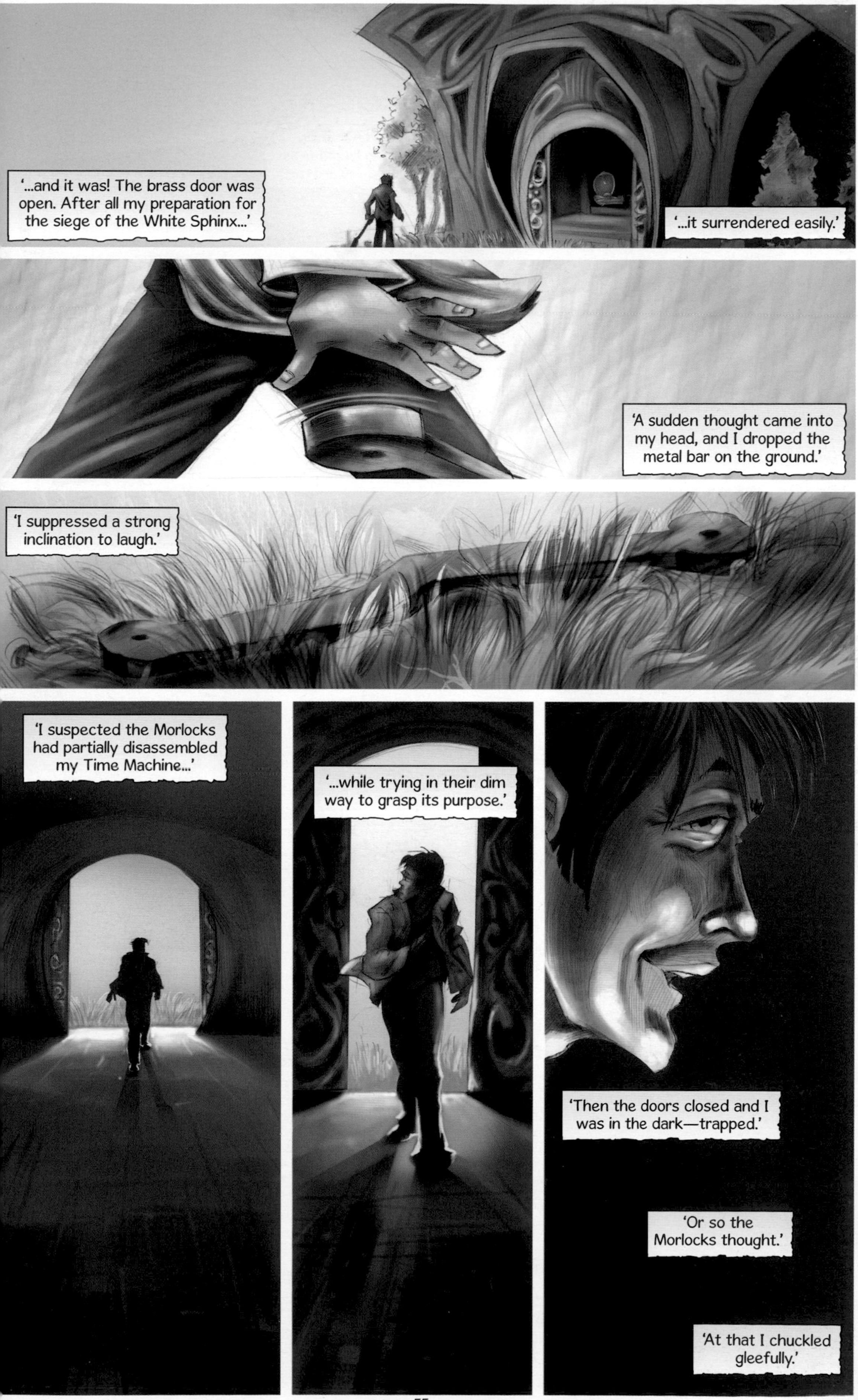
'...and it was! The brass door was open. After all my preparation for the siege of the White Sphinx...'
'...it surrendered easily.'
'A sudden thought came into my head, and I dropped the metal bar on the ground.'
'I suppressed a strong inclination to laugh.'
'I suspected the Morlocks had partially disassembled my Time Machine...'
'...while trying in their dim way to grasp its purpose.'
'Then the doors closed and I was in the dark—trapped.'
'Or so the Morlocks thought.'
'At that I chuckled gleefully.'

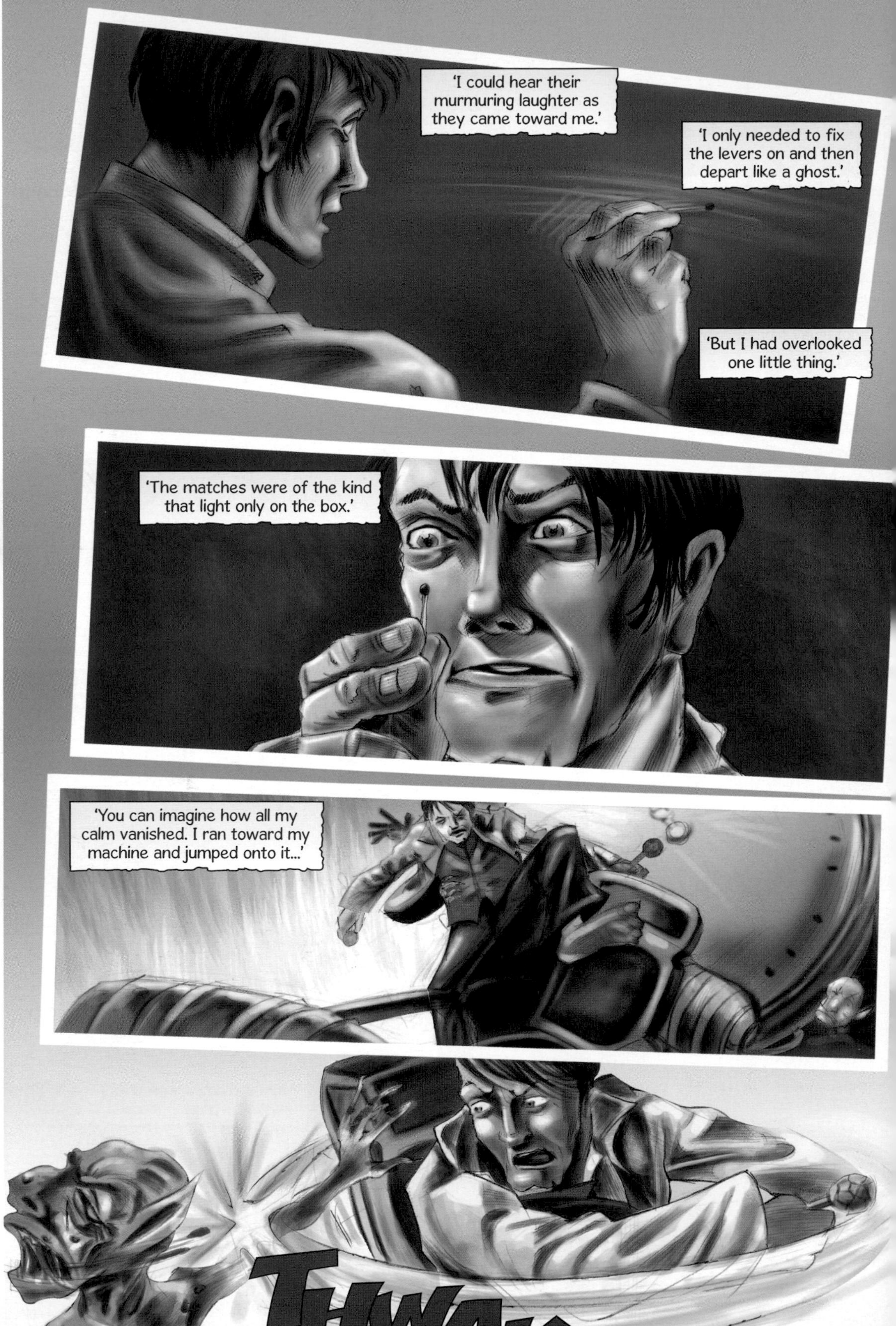

'I could hear their murmuring laughter as they came toward me.'
'I only needed to fix the levers on and then depart like a ghost.'
'But I had overlooked one little thing.'
'The matches were of the kind that light only on the box.'
'You can imagine how all my calm vanished. I ran toward my machine and jumped onto it...'
THWAK
'...fighting all those ugly creatures who came my way.'

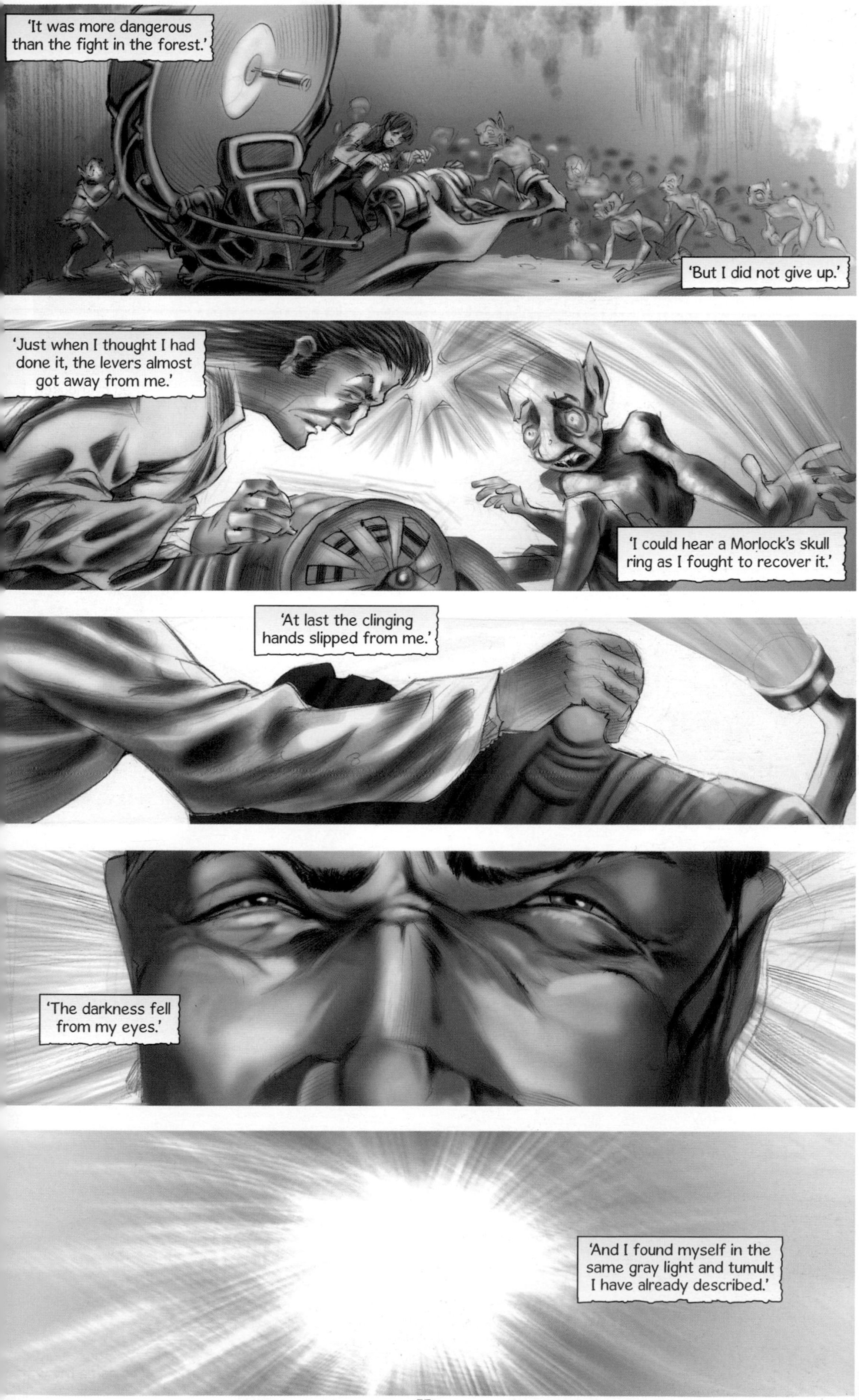
'It was more dangerous than the fight in the forest.'
'But I did not give up.'
'Just when I thought I had done it, the levers almost got away from me.'
'I could hear a Morlock's skull ring as I fought to recover it.'
'At last the clinging hands slipped from me.'
'The darkness fell from my eyes.'
'And I found myself in the same gray light and tumult I have already described.'

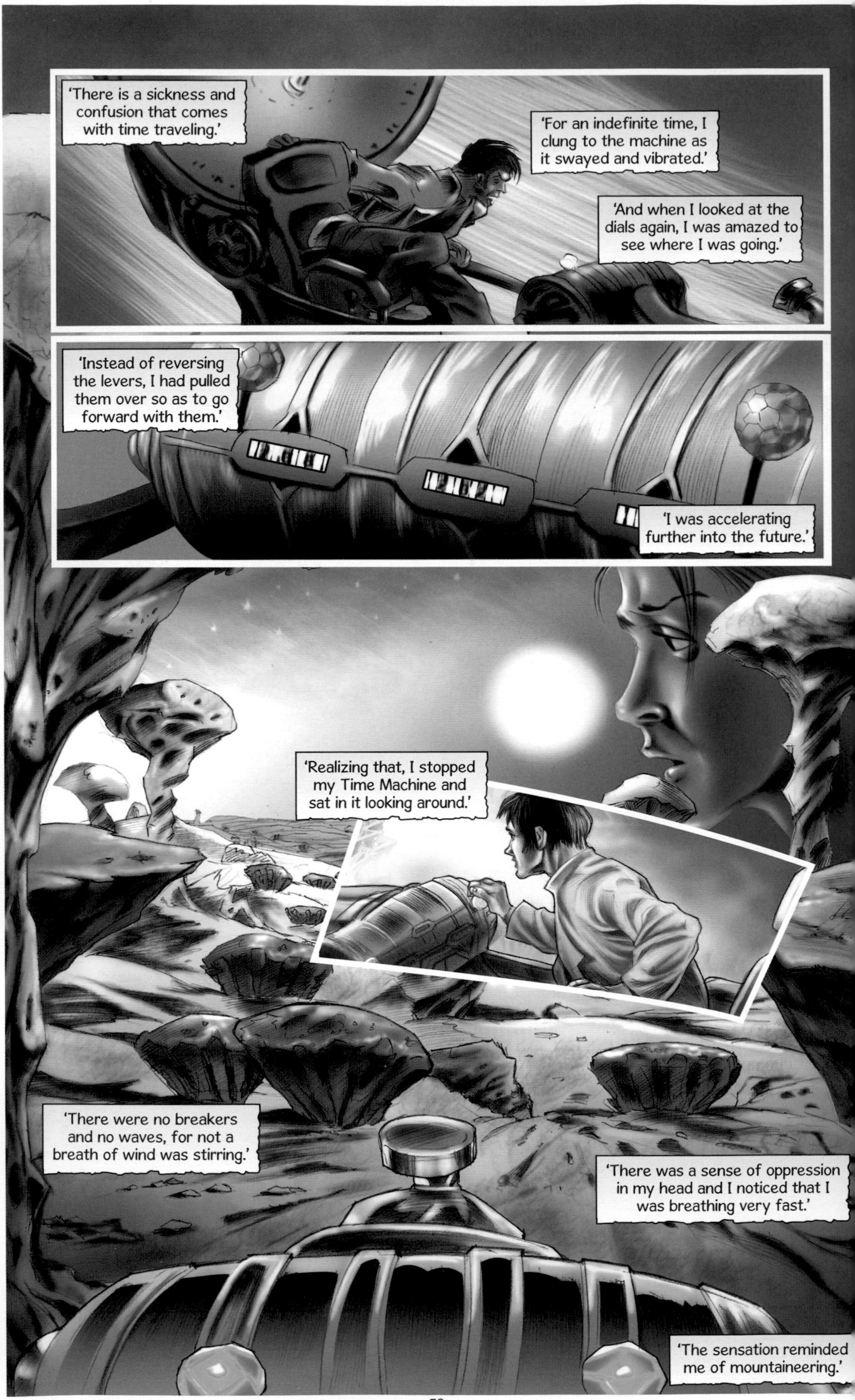
'There is a sickness and confusion that comes with time traveling.'
'For an indefinite time, I clung to the machine as it swayed and vibrated.'
'And when I looked at the dials again, I was amazed to see where I was going.'
'Instead of reversing the levers, I had pulled them over so as to go forward with them.'
'I was accelerating further into the future.'
'Realizing that, I stopped my Time Machine and sat in it looking around.'
'There were no breakers and no waves, for not a breath of wind was stirring.'
'There was a sense of oppression in my head and I noticed that I was breathing very fast.'
'The sensation reminded me of mountaineering.'

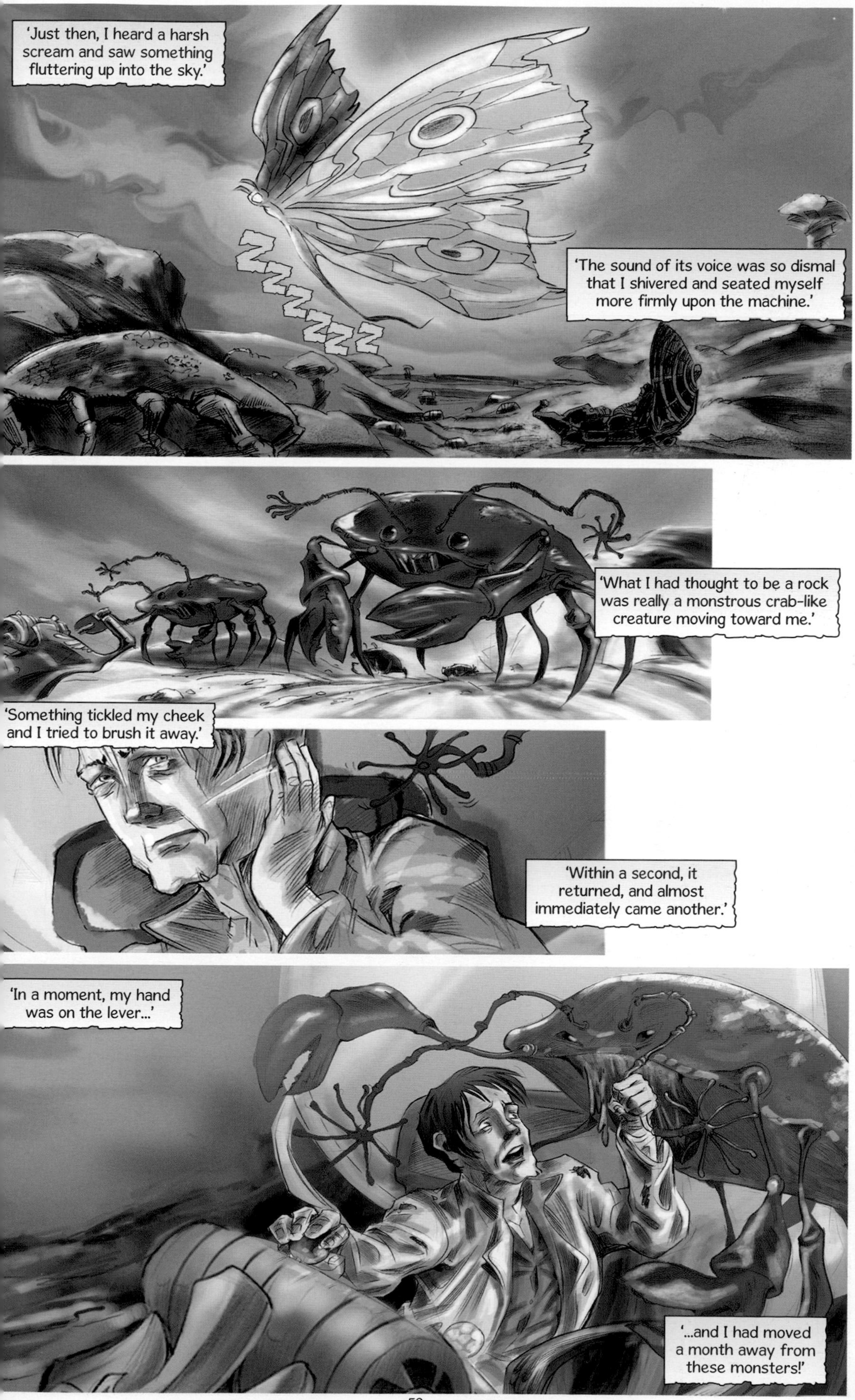
'Just then, I heard a harsh scream and saw something fluttering up into the sky.'
ZZZZZZZ
'The sound of its voice was so dismal that I shivered and seated myself more firmly upon the machine.'
'What I had thought to be a rock was really a monstrous crab-like creature moving toward me.'
'Something tickled my cheek and I tried to brush it away.'
'Within a second, it returned, and almost immediately came another.'
'In a moment, my hand was on the lever...'
'...and I had moved a month away from these monsters!'

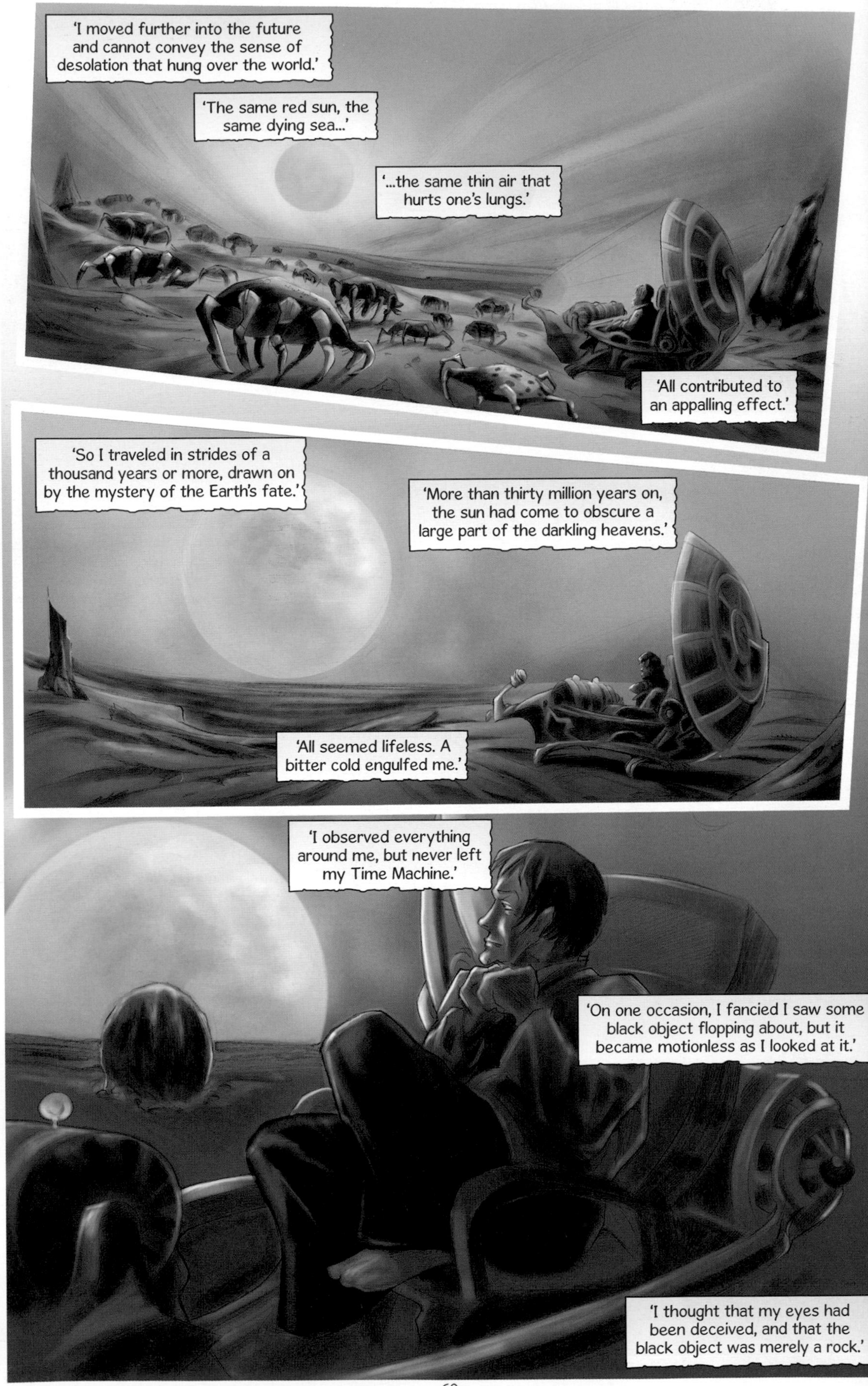
'I moved further into the future and cannot convey the sense of desolation that hung over the world.'
'The same red sun, the same dying sea...'
'...the same thin air that hurts one's lungs.'
'All contributed to an appalling effect.'
'So I traveled in strides of a thousand years or more, drawn on by the mystery of the Earth's fate.'
'More than thirty million years on, the sun had come to obscure a large part of the darkling heavens.'
'All seemed lifeless. A bitter cold engulfed me.'
'I observed everything around me, but never left my Time Machine.'
'On one occasion, I fancied I saw some black object flopping about, but it became motionless as I looked at it.'
'I thought that my eyes had been deceived, and that the black object was merely a rock.'

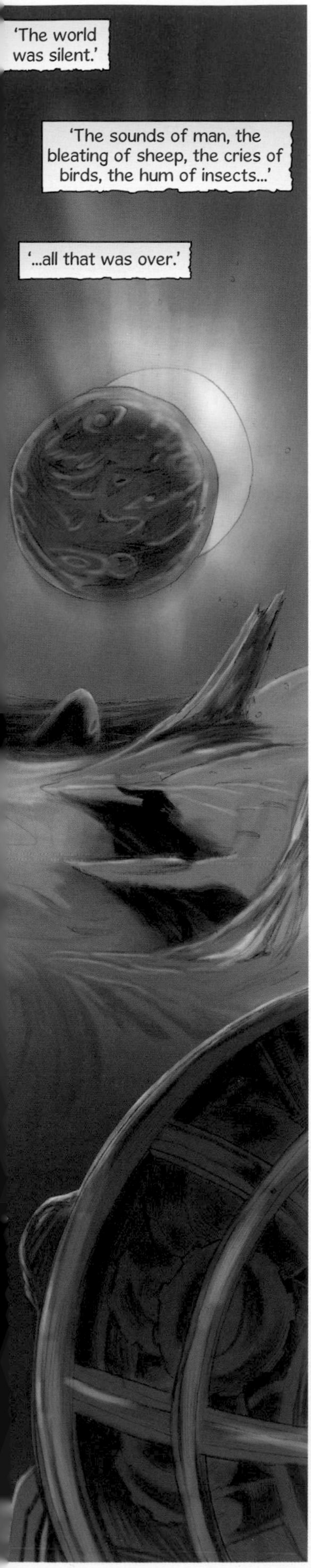
'The world was silent.'
'The sounds of man, the bleating of sheep, the cries of birds, the hum of insects...'
'...all that was over.'

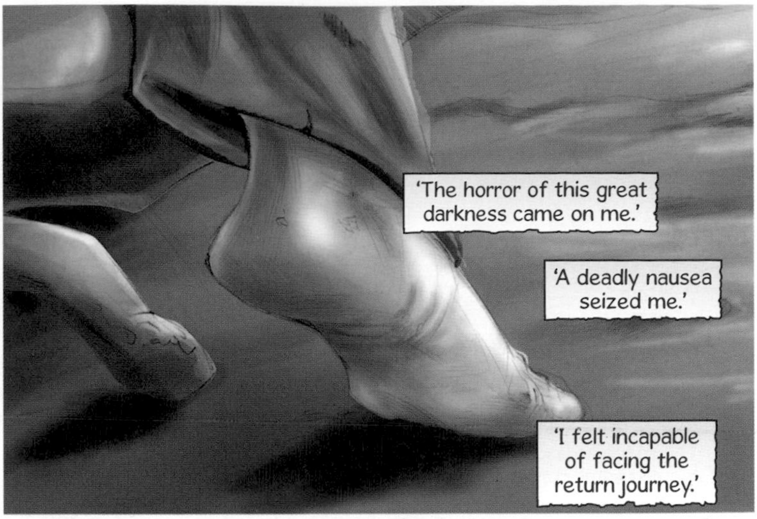
'The horror of this great darkness came on me.'
'A deadly nausea seized me.'
'I felt incapable of facing the return journey.'

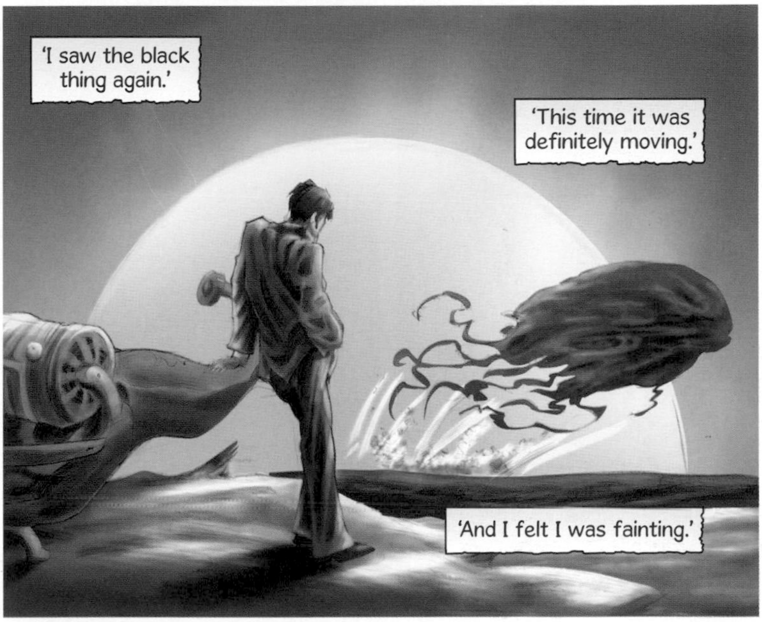
'I saw the black thing again.'
'This time it was definitely moving.'
'And I felt I was fainting.'

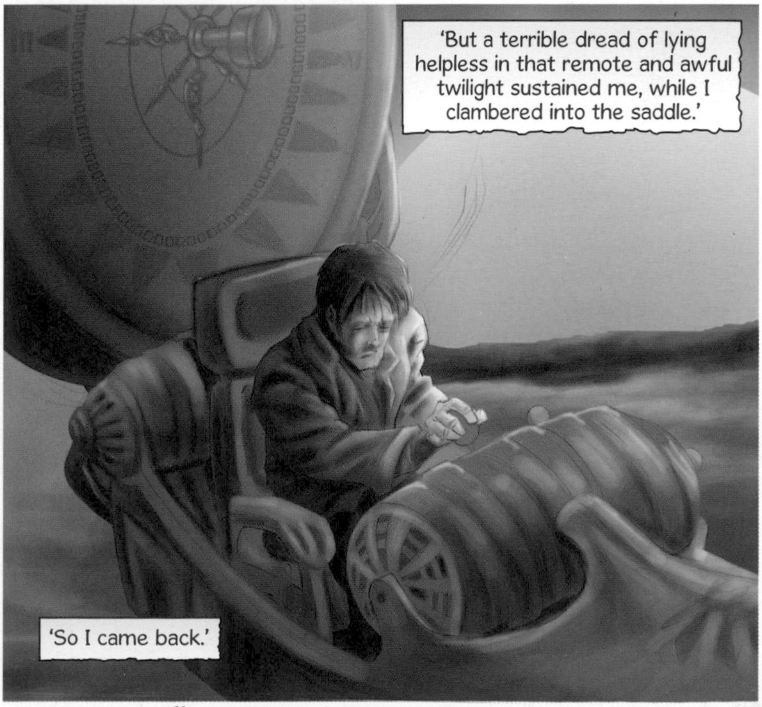
'But a terrible dread of lying helpless in that remote and awful twilight sustained me, while I clambered into the saddle.'
'So I came back.'

'At last I saw the dim shadows of houses again; the evidences of corrupt humanity.'

'I saw the old familiar laboratory around me, exactly as it had been.'

'And yet, not exactly!'

'The machine had stopped in a different corner from where it started...'

I cannot expect you to believe it.

Take it as a lie, or a prophecy, or say I dreamed it.

But if you take it as a story, what do you think of it?

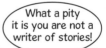

What a pity it is you are not a writer of stories!

You do not believe it? I hardly believe it myself.

And yet...

'...the exact distance between the little lawn and the pedestal of the White Sphinx, into which the Morlocks had carried my machine.'

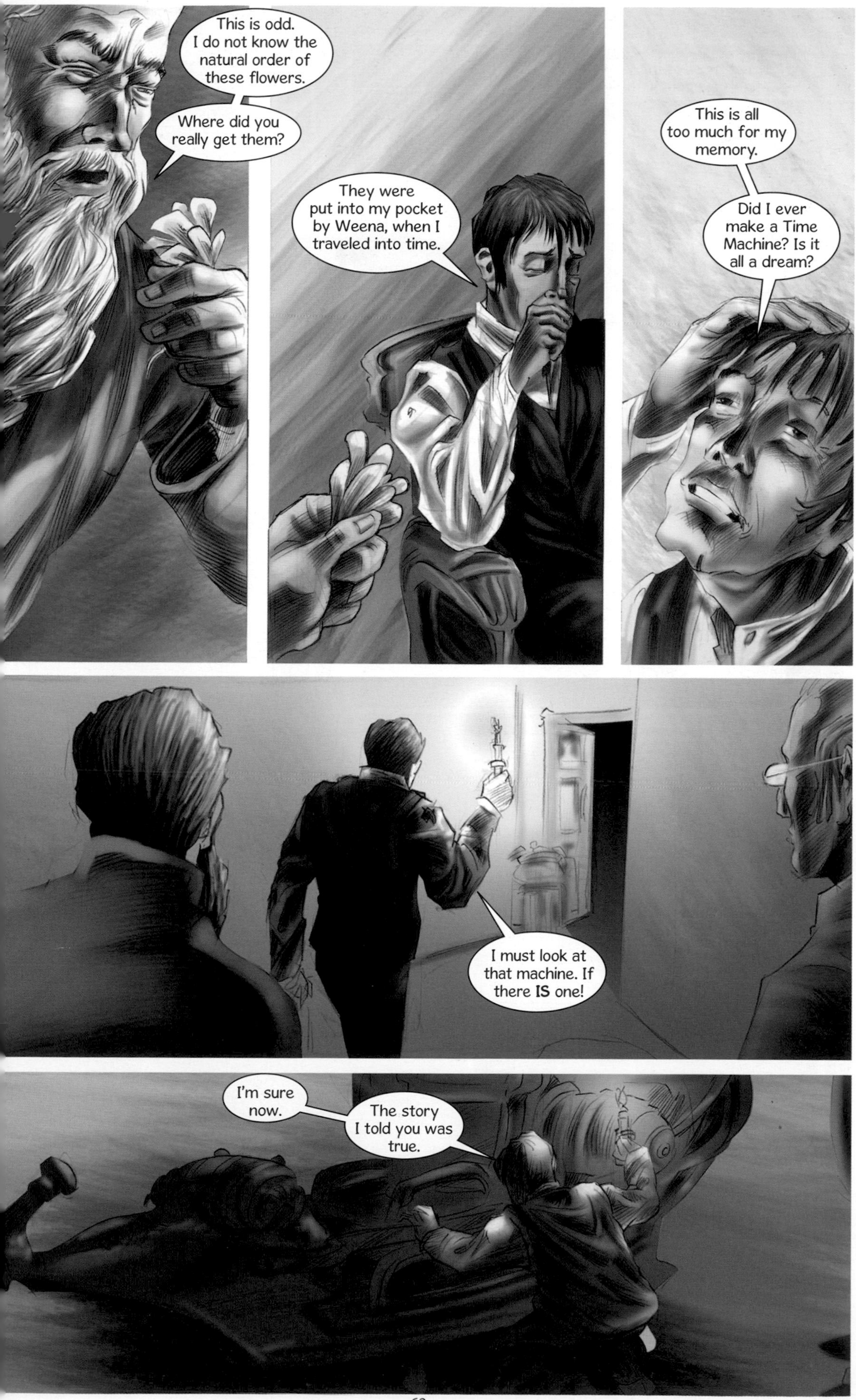

This is odd. I do not know the natural order of these flowers.
Where did you really get them?
They were put into my pocket by Weena, when I traveled into time.
This is all too much for my memory.
Did I ever make a Time Machine? Is it all a dream?
I must look at that machine. If there **IS** one!
I'm sure now.
The story I told you was true.

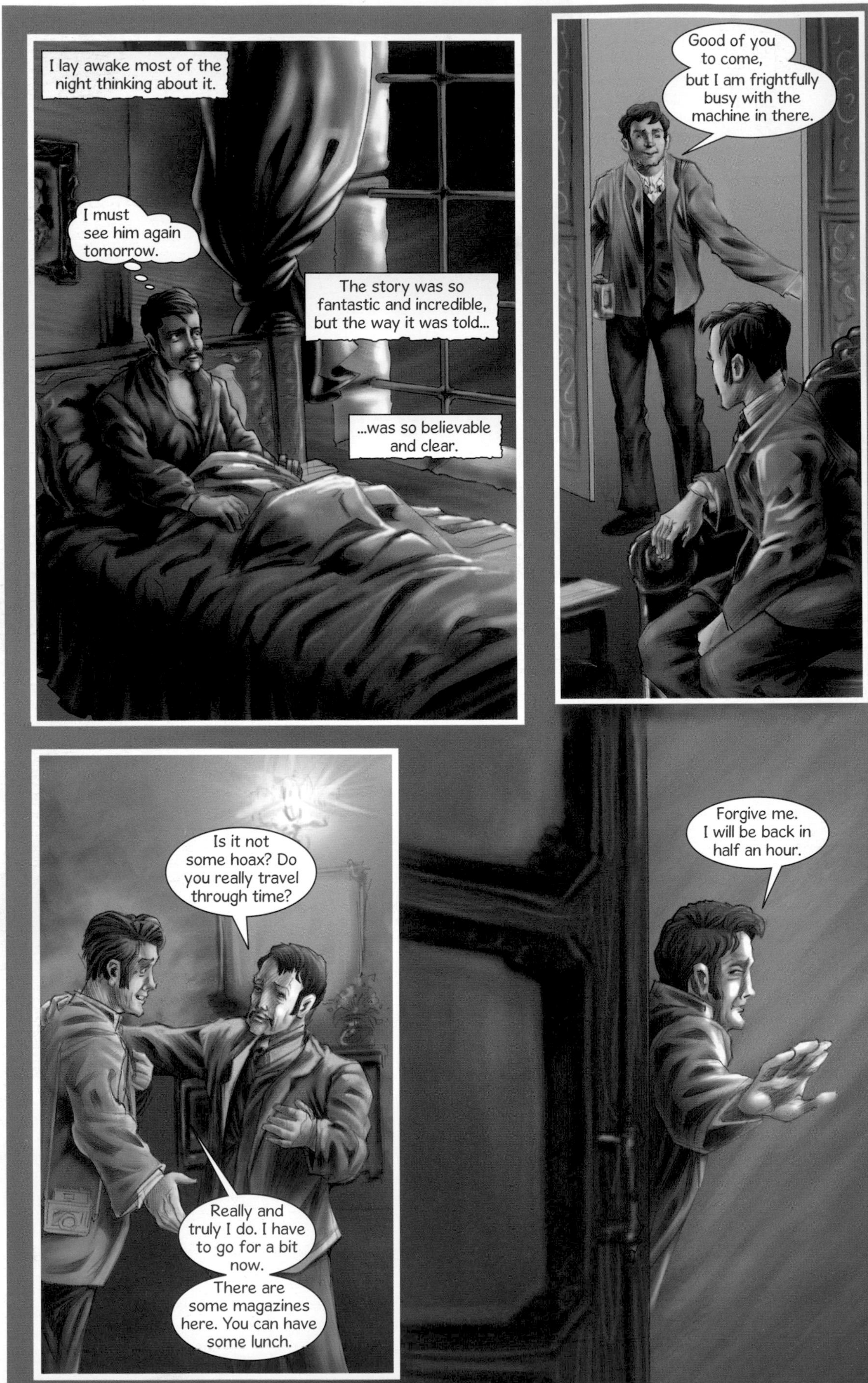
I lay awake most of the night thinking about it.
I must see him again tomorrow.
The story was so fantastic and incredible, but the way it was told...
...was so believable and clear.
Good of you to come, but I am frightfully busy with the machine in there.
Is it not some hoax? Do you really travel through time?
Really and truly I do. I have to go for a bit now.
There are some magazines here. You can have some lunch.
Forgive me. I will be back in half an hour.

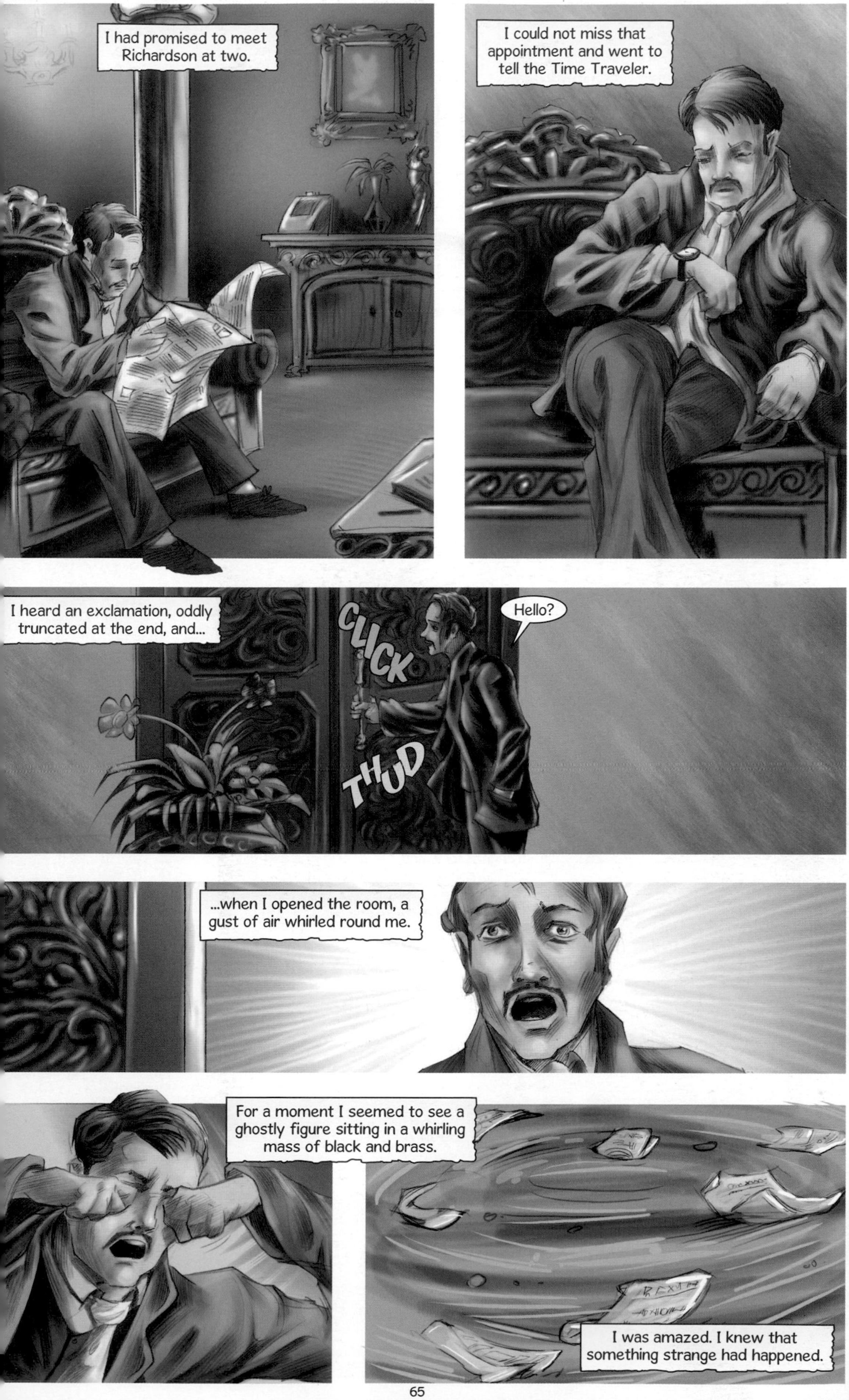
I had promised to meet Richardson at two.
I could not miss that appointment and went to tell the Time Traveler.
I heard an exclamation, oddly truncated at the end, and...
CLICK
Hello?
THUD
...when I opened the room, a gust of air whirled round me.
For a moment I seemed to see a ghostly figure sitting in a whirling mass of black and brass.
I was amazed. I knew that something strange had happened.

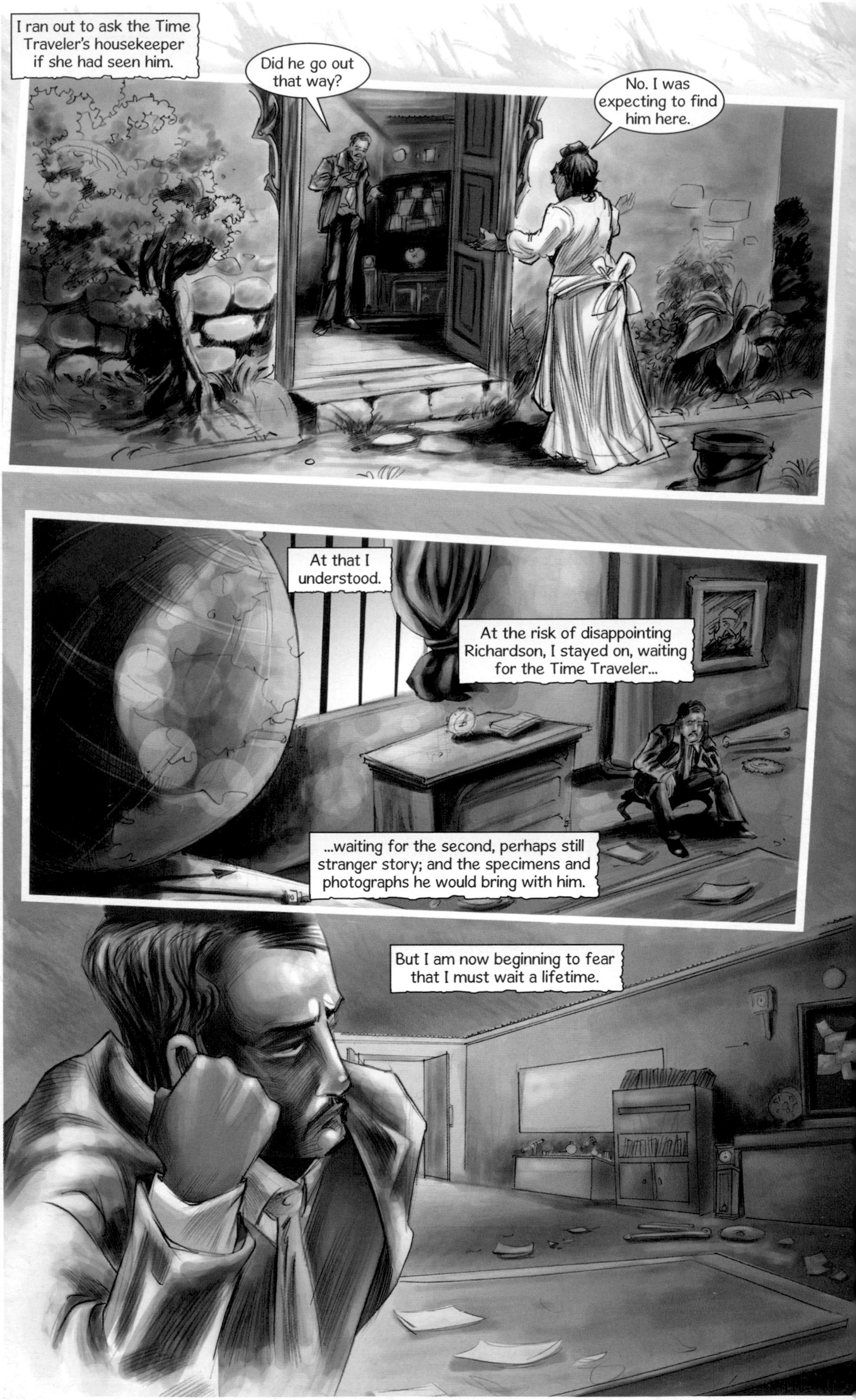

I ran out to ask the Time Traveler's housekeeper if she had seen him.
Did he go out that way?
No. I was expecting to find him here.
At that I understood.
At the risk of disappointing Richardson, I stayed on, waiting for the Time Traveler...
...waiting for the second, perhaps still stranger story; and the specimens and photographs he would bring with him.
But I am now beginning to fear that I must wait a lifetime.

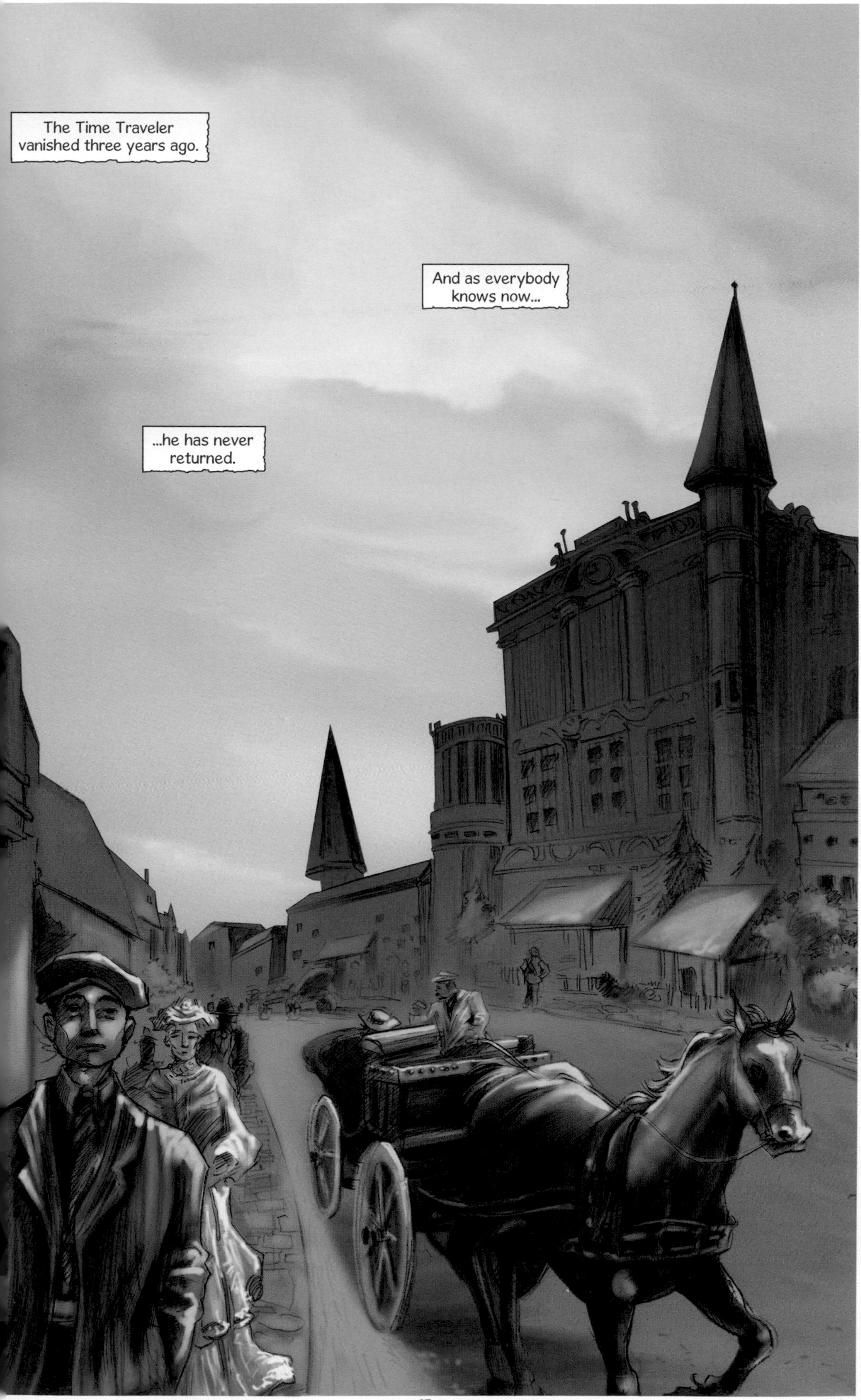
The Time Traveler vanished three years ago.
And as everybody knows now...
...he has never returned.

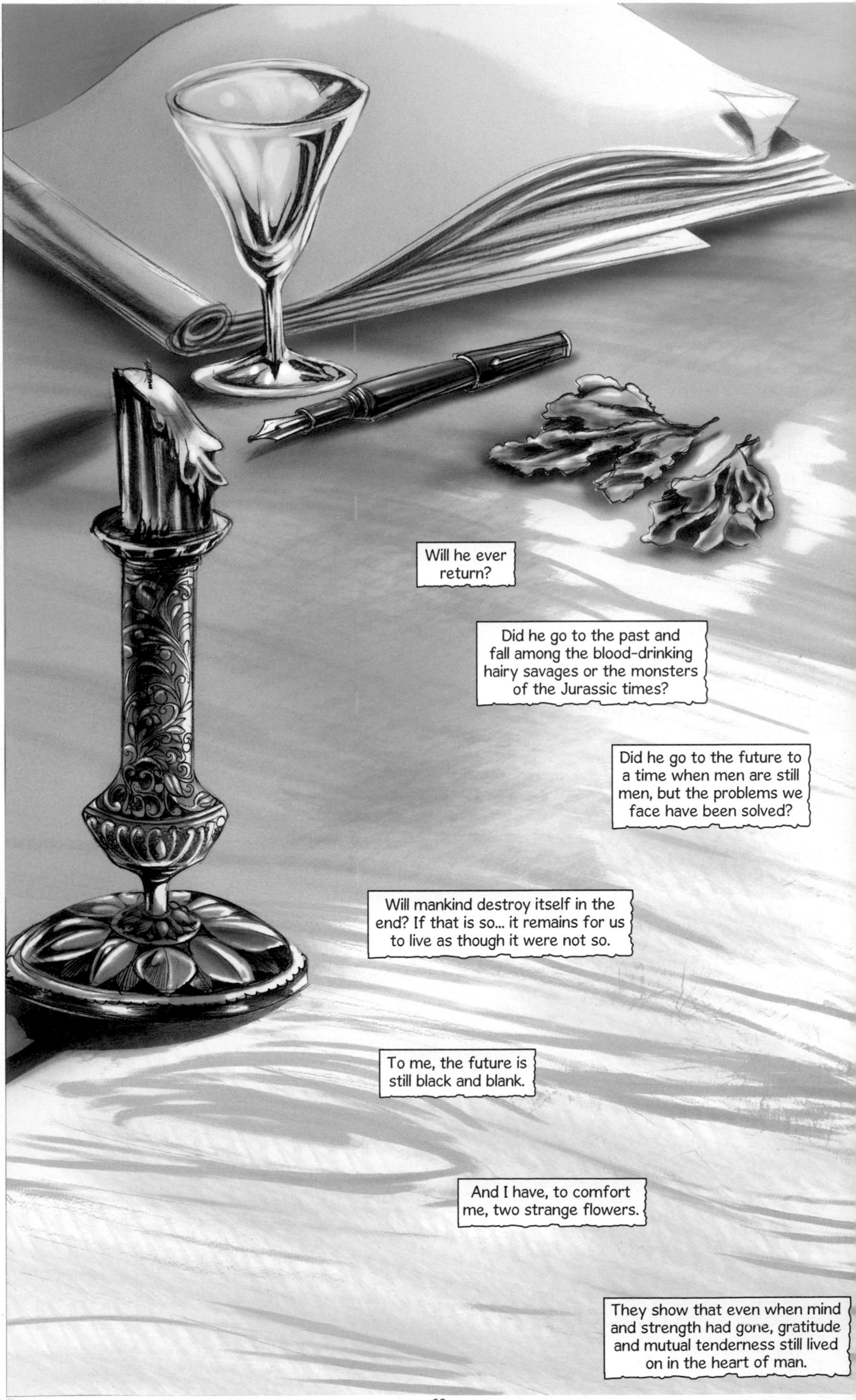

Will he ever return?
Did he go to the past and fall among the blood-drinking hairy savages or the monsters of the Jurassic times?
Did he go to the future to a time when men are still men, but the problems we face have been solved?
Will mankind destroy itself in the end? If that is so... it remains for us to live as though it were not so.
To me, the future is still black and blank.
And I have, to comfort me, two strange flowers.
They show that even when mind and strength had gone, gratitude and mutual tenderness still lived on in the heart of man.

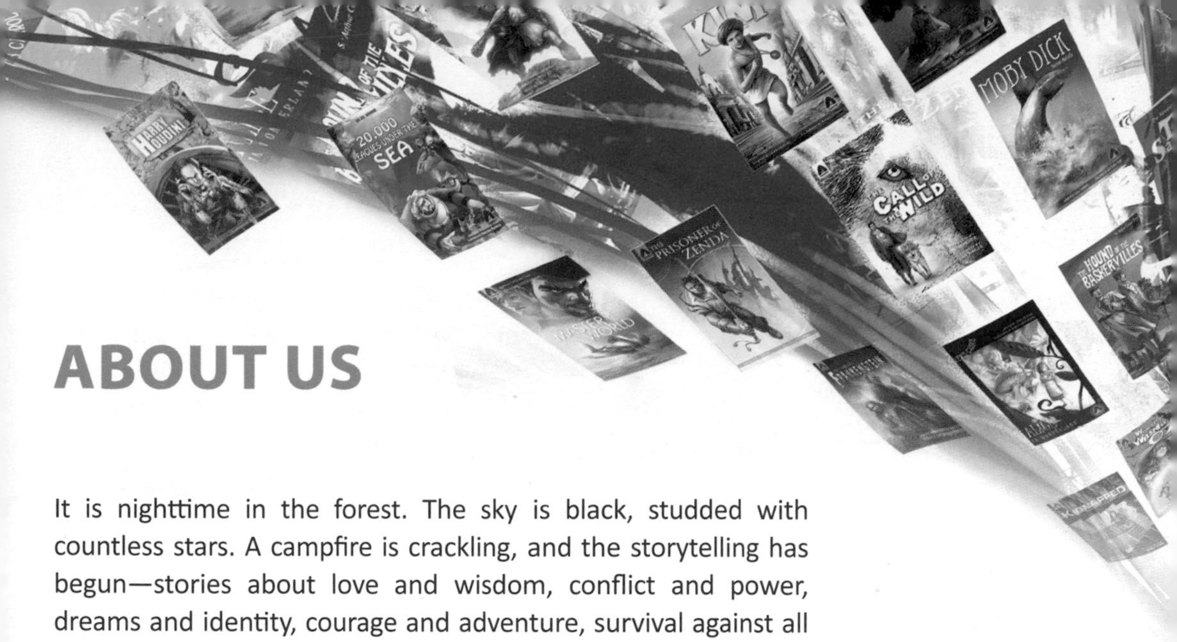
HARRY HOUDINI
20,000 LEAGUES UNDER THE SEA
MOBY DICK
THE CALL OF THE WILD
THE PRISONER OF ZENDA
THE HOUND OF THE BASKERVILLES
KIDNAPPED

ABOUT US

It is nighttime in the forest. The sky is black, studded with countless stars. A campfire is crackling, and the storytelling has begun—stories about love and wisdom, conflict and power, dreams and identity, courage and adventure, survival against all odds, and hope against all hope. In the warm, cheerful radiance of the campfire, the storyteller's audience is captivated, as in a trance. Even the trees and the earth and the animals of the forest seem to have fallen silent, bewitched.

Inspired by this enduring relationship between a campfire and gripping storytelling, we bring you four series of *Campfire Graphic Novels*:

Our *Classic* tales adapt timeless literature from some of the greatest writers ever.

Our *Mythology* series features epics, myths and legends from around the world; tales that transport readers to lands of mystery and magic.

Our *Biography* titles bring to life remarkable and inspiring figures from history.

Our *Original* line showcases brand new characters and stories from some of today's most talented graphic novelists and illustrators.

We hope you will gather around our campfire and discover the fascinating stories and characters inside our books.

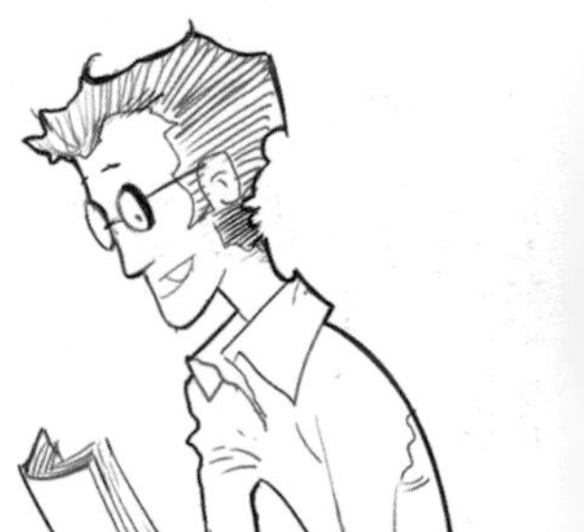

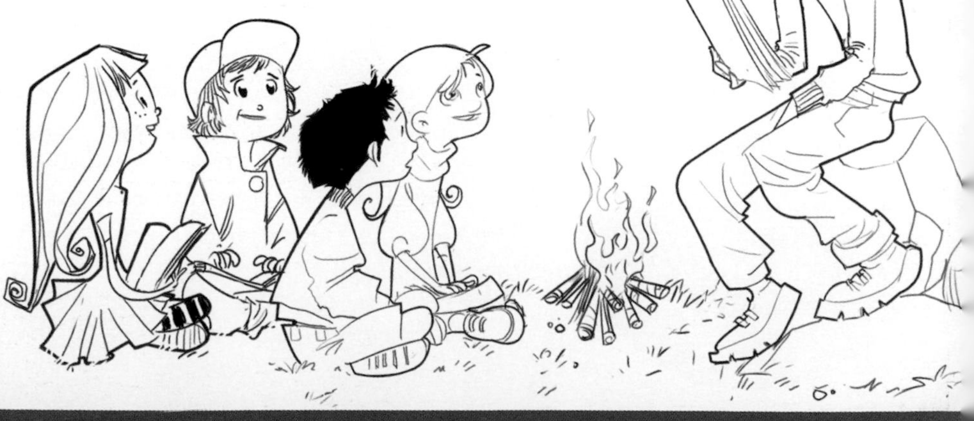

CAMPFIRE™

H. G. WELLS'S NOVEL *THE TIME MACHINE* WAS FIRST PUBLISHED IN 1895. WHAT WERE SOME OF THE REAL-WORLD DISCOVERIES AND INVENTIONS THAT WERE SEEING THE LIGHT OF DAY AROUND THIS TIME? HERE WE TAKE A LOOK AT SOME OF THE EXCITING NEW TECHNOLOGICAL BREAKTHROUGHS OF THE LATE 19TH AND EARLY 20TH CENTURIES.

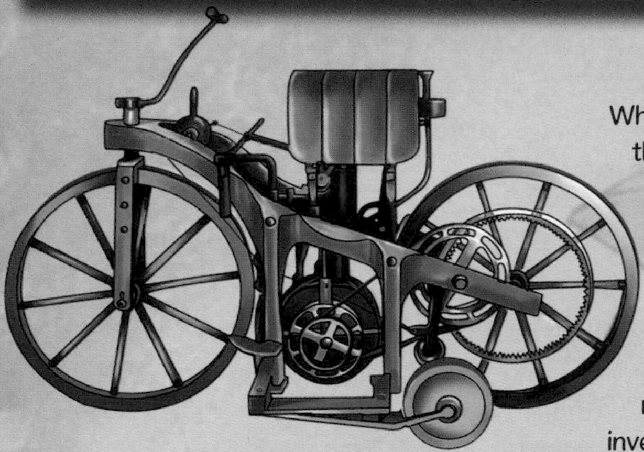

MOTORCYCLE

When you think of a motorcycle today, the image that probably comes to your mind is that of a Harley-Davidson cruising on a highway. However, the earliest motorcycle was actually developed in 1867 by an American inventor called Sylvester Howard Roper. His two-cylinder motorcycle included a steam engine powered by coal! The first gas engine motorcycle was invented by the German inventor Gottlieb Daimler in 1885. It is interesting to note that the gas-powered engine that Daimler used in his mostly wooden motorcycle was invented by Nicolaus August Otto, and was called the 'Otto Cycle Engine'.

PHONOGRAPH

In an age when we carry our media in our pockets, listening to music on our MP3 players and mobile phones, it is easy to forget that reproducing recorded sound was a significant invention of the 20th century. The invention of the phonograph is generally credited to the American inventor Thomas Edison. How did Edison's phonograph (pictured here) work? It consisted of tinfoil wrapped around a cylinder and a vibrating stylus that embossed indentations, or recordings, into the sheet of tinfoil as the cylinder rotated.

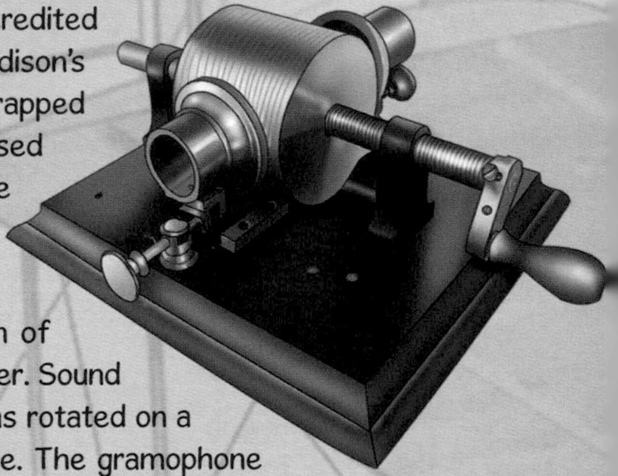

However, it wasn't until 1887, ten years after Edison's tinfoil phonograph, that Émile Berliner patented his innovation of recording on a flat disk or record, rather than on a cylinder. Sound grooves were etched into a flat record, which in turn was rotated on a reproducing machine. Berliner named this a Gramophone. The gramophone arm held a needle that read the grooves in the record by vibration and transmitted the information to the gramophone speaker.

RECORD

Émile Berliner's flat discs, or 'records', were the first sound recordings that could be mass-produced. A negative was made from the flat master disc, and the negative was then used as a mold for making copies that reproduced the original master disc.

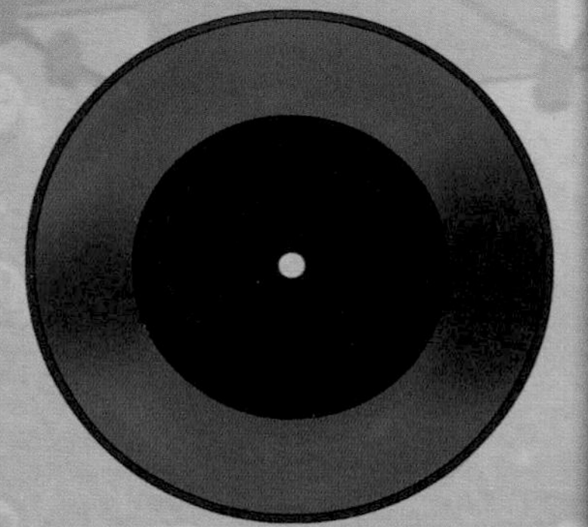

DID YOU KNOW?

- 1915: THE 78-RPM (REVOLUTIONS PER MINUTE) RECORD BECAME STANDARD, WITH A PLAYING TIME OF ABOUT 4½ MINUTES PER SIDE.
- 1948: COLUMBIA RECORDS INTRODUCED THE LONG-PLAYING (LP) RECORD, WHICH, WITH A ROTATIONAL SPEED OF 33.3 RPM AND THE USE OF VERY FINE GROOVES, HAD A PLAYING TIME OF 30 MINUTES PER SIDE. SOON AFTER, RCA CORPORATION INTRODUCED 45-RPM DISCS ('SINGLES') WITH A PLAYING TIME OF UP TO 8 MINUTES PER SIDE.
- 1980s: RECORDED CASSETTES AND COMPACT DISCS (CDs) LARGELY SUPPLANTED RECORDS AS THE CHIEF MEANS OF REPRODUCING RECORDED SOUND AT HOME.

X-RAY

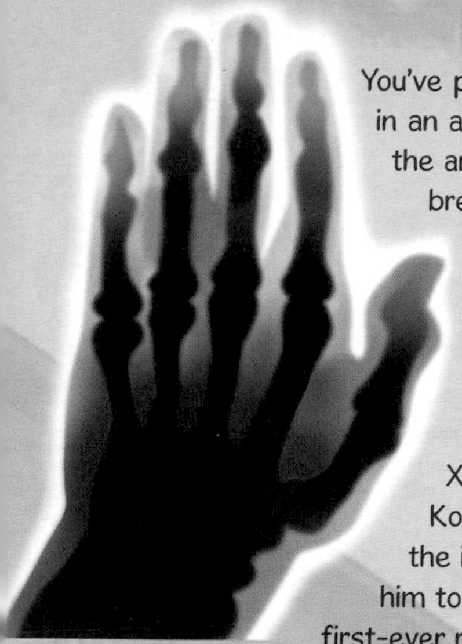

You've probably heard the term X-ray being used in a doctor's office or in an airport. X-rays are widely used by doctors and surgeons to study the architecture of bones and other soft tissues, to ensure there is no breakage or abnormal growth in them. They are also used to examine baggage and cargo to prevent illegal transportation of goods.

Another important use of X-rays is in the detection of structural problems in metal objects, and in monitoring the effects of stress in materials that are used in the construction of skyscrapers, bridges and aircraft.

X-rays were discovered by a German physicist called Wilhelm Konrad von Roentgen in 1895. This high-energy radiation revealed the internal structures of the materials it passed through and allowed him to photograph them! For this achievement, Roentgen was made the first-ever recipient of the Nobel Prize for Physics in 1901.

DID YOU KNOW?

- THESE RAYS WERE LABELED WITH AN 'X' BECAUSE THERE WAS SO LITTLE KNOWN ABOUT THEM AT THE TIME OF THEIR DISCOVERY!
- MOVIES BASED ON THE SUPERHERO SUPERMAN HAVE SHOWN HIM TO HAVE X-RAY VISION!
- LUXRAY, A CHARACTER FROM THE POKÉMON SERIES, ALSO HAS X-RAY VISION, TO SPOT PREY HIDING BEHIND OBJECTS!

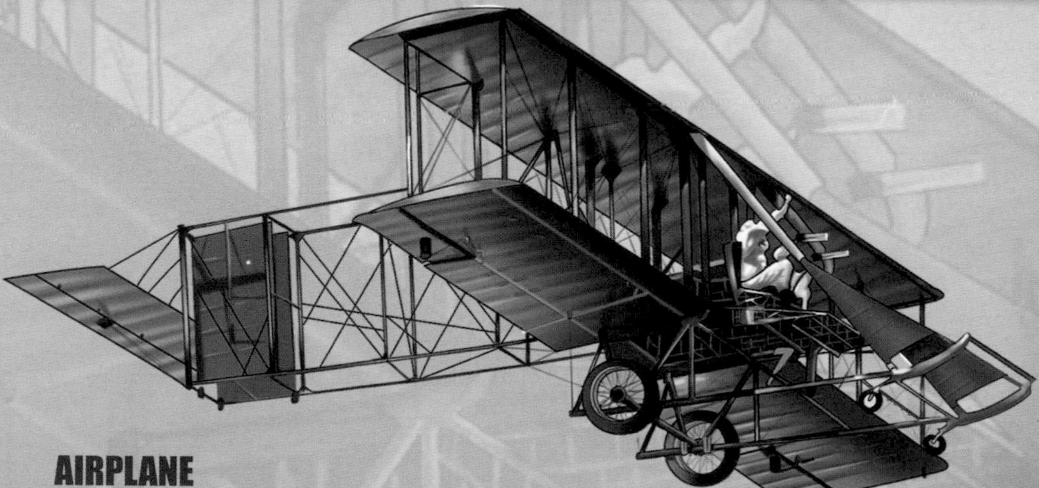

AIRPLANE

Today, air travel has become a common fact of life. But when you see an airplane, do you ever wonder about the dreamers and visionaries who made human flight possible?

The Wright brothers—Wilbur and Orville—are credited for not only inventing and building the first successful airplane, but also for making the first powered human flight. On December 17, 1903, in a place called Kitty Hawk, in the American state of North Carolina, the Wright brothers' Flyer made a 12 second flight with Orville at the controls. As we all know, the world has never been the same since.

How did two unknown Americans, running a modest bicycle business, create what Leonardo da Vinci had imagined centuries before them? The Wright brothers had a grand dream, but it was their creativity, determination and perseverance that led them to apply scientific methodology and single-handedly develop the technologies to make their dream come true.

With the realization of their dream, the Wright brothers ultimately helped to bring people, ideas, cultures and businesses together, making the world a much smaller place.